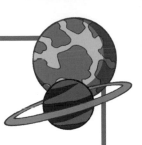

To
LUCAS

THE ADVENTURES OF

JONNIE ROCKET

'LIVE YOUR DREAMS'

THE ORIGINAL

John Chapman (signature)

Author and creator John Chapman

Illustrations by The Comic Stripper Studio

A CIP catalogue record of this book is available from the British Library

ISBN: 978-0-9573035-0-8

Published by Jonnie Rocket Ltd. 2013

Printed by DCW Penrose & Co. Ltd. Staines, Middlesex

First edition: 2000
Second edition: 2008
Third edition: 2013

www.jonnierocket.com

Meet the Cast!

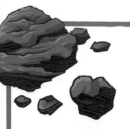

Jonnie Rocket

Mum

Dad

Grandma

Sam the spider

Jonnie's bike, Tycho

Captain Downfall

Bosun Duped

Zip and Zap

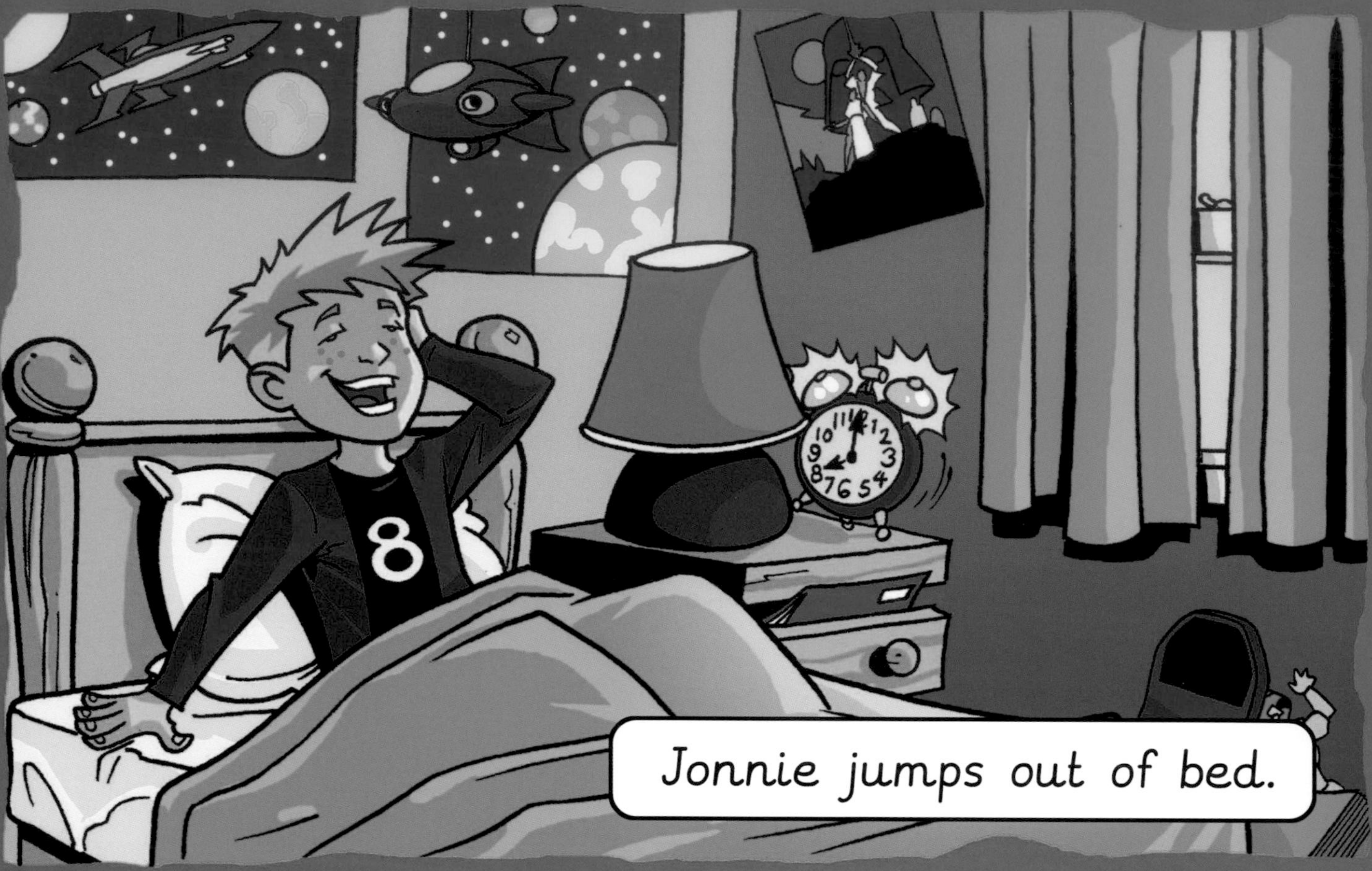
Jonnie jumps out of bed.

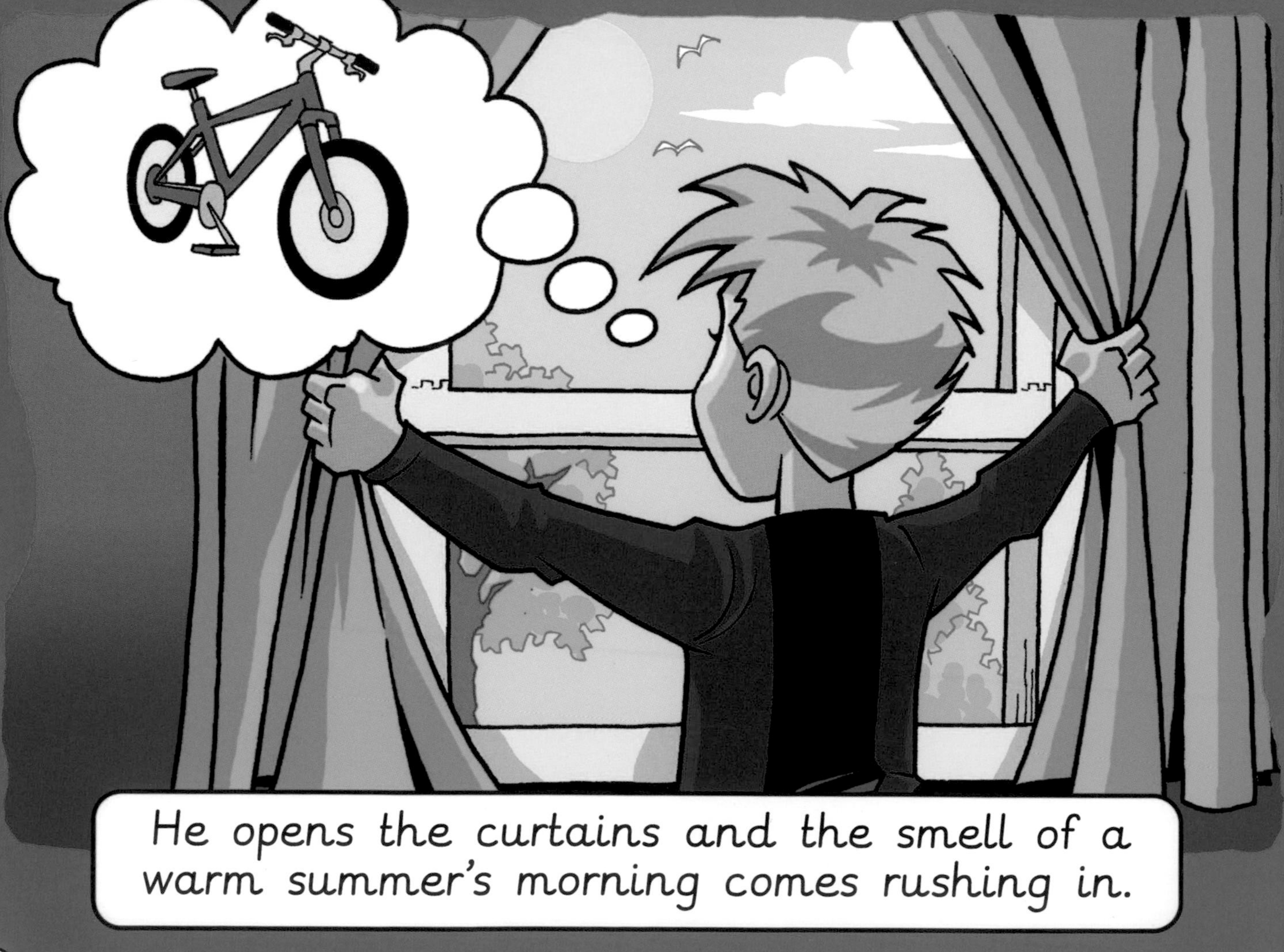
He opens the curtains and the smell of a warm summer's morning comes rushing in.

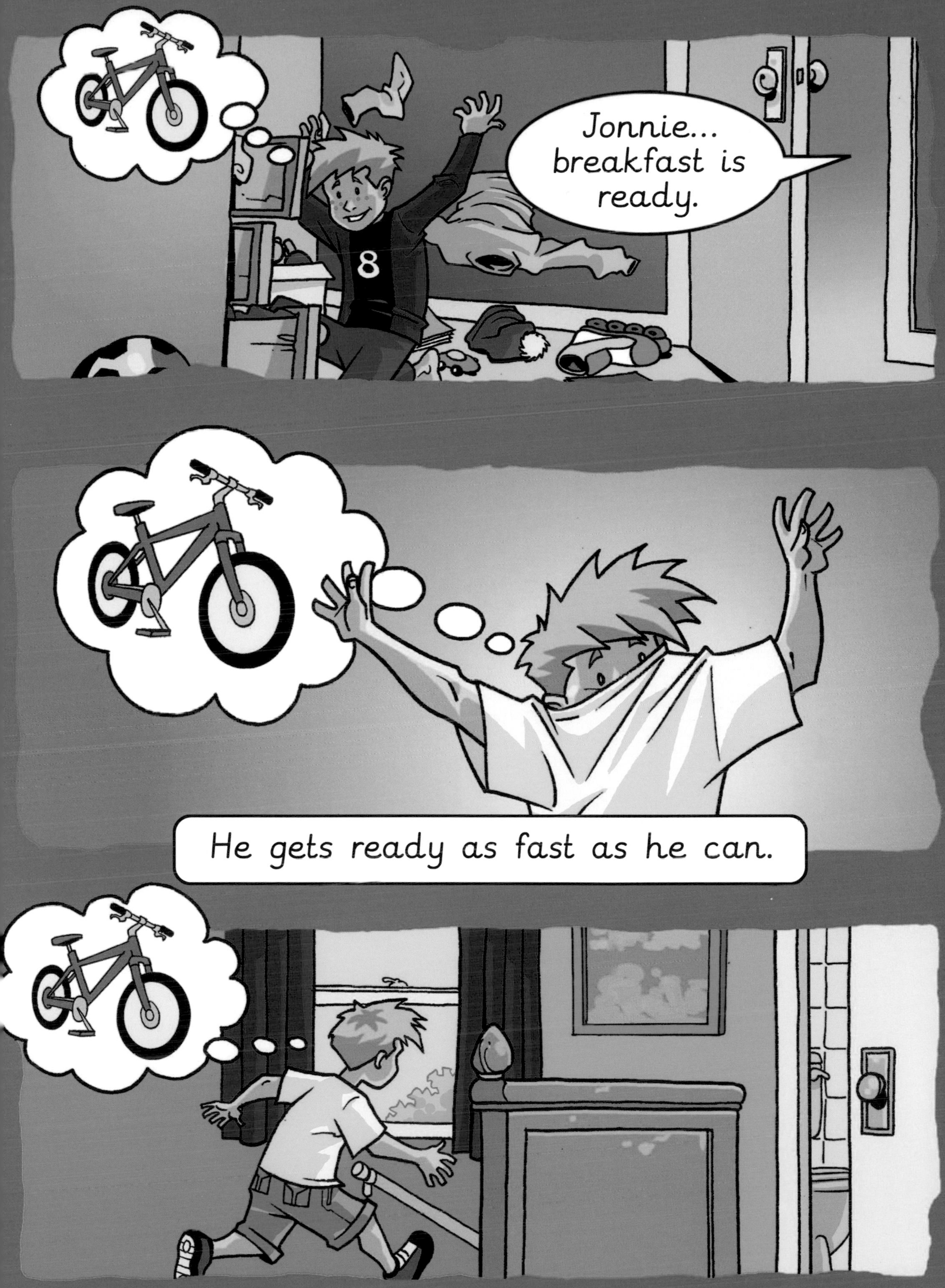

Jonnie...
breakfast is
ready.
He gets ready as fast as he can.

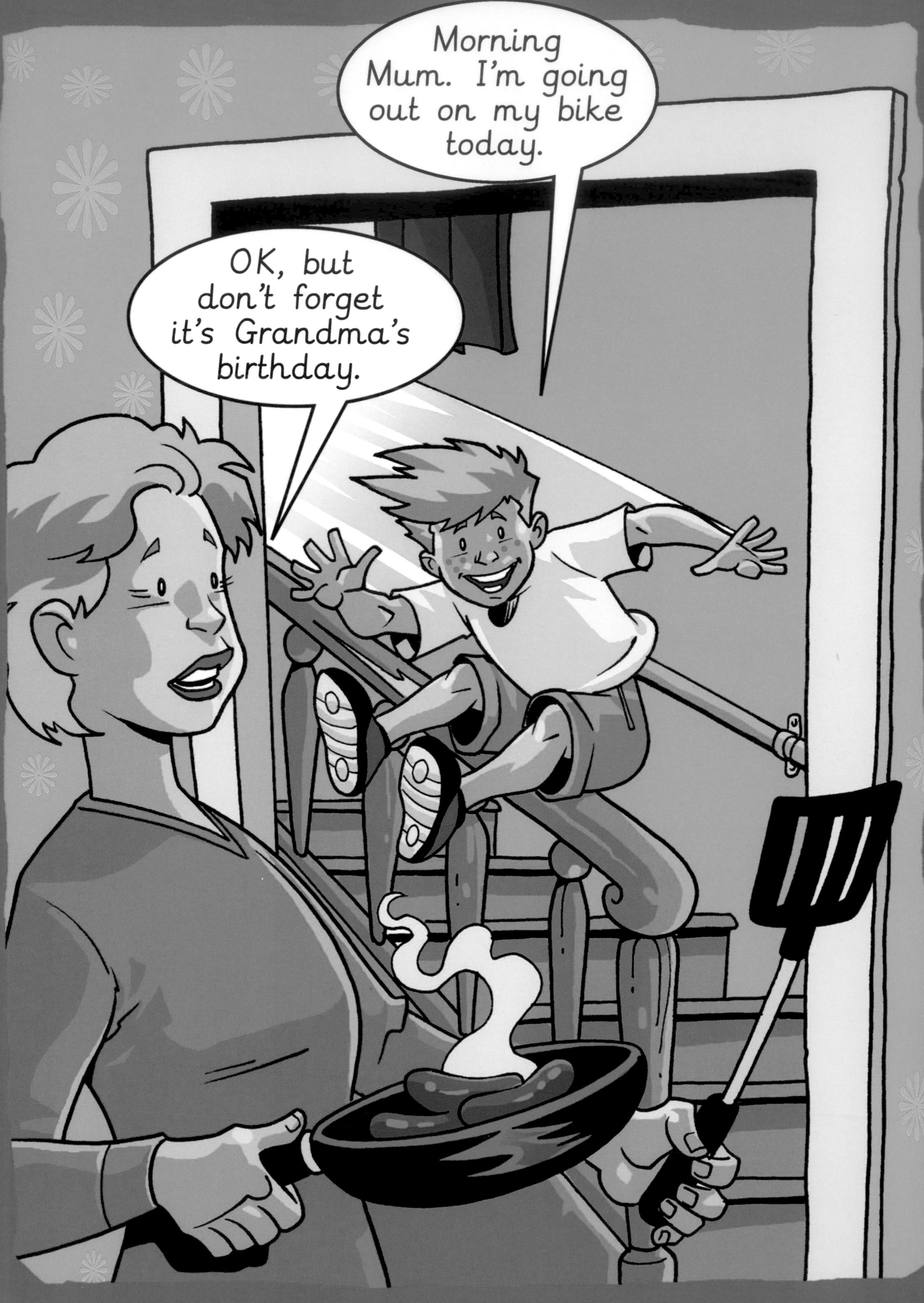
Morning Mum. I'm going out on my bike today.
OK, but don't forget it's Grandma's birthday.

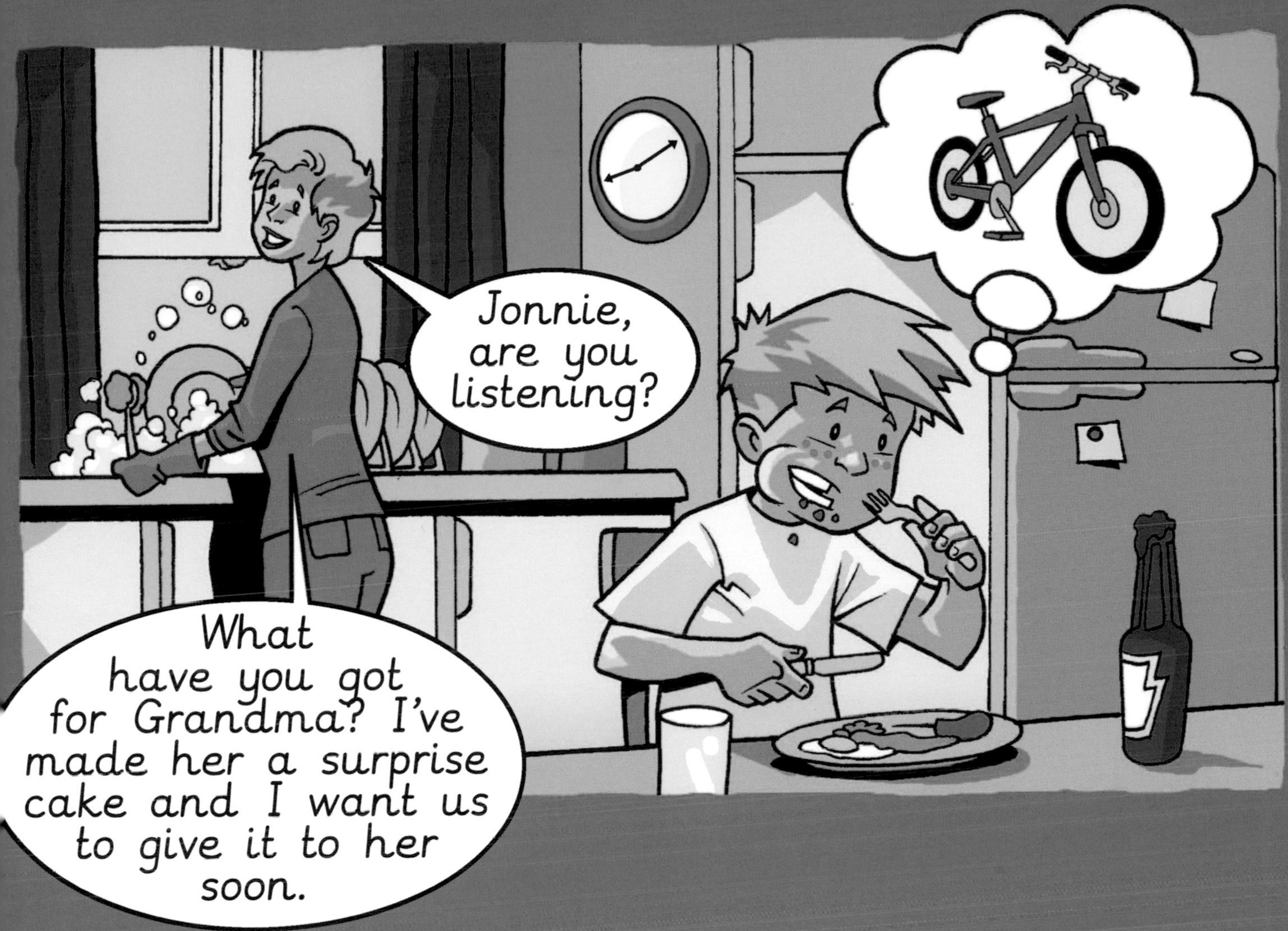
Jonnie, are you listening?
What have you got for Grandma? I've made her a surprise cake and I want us to give it to her soon.

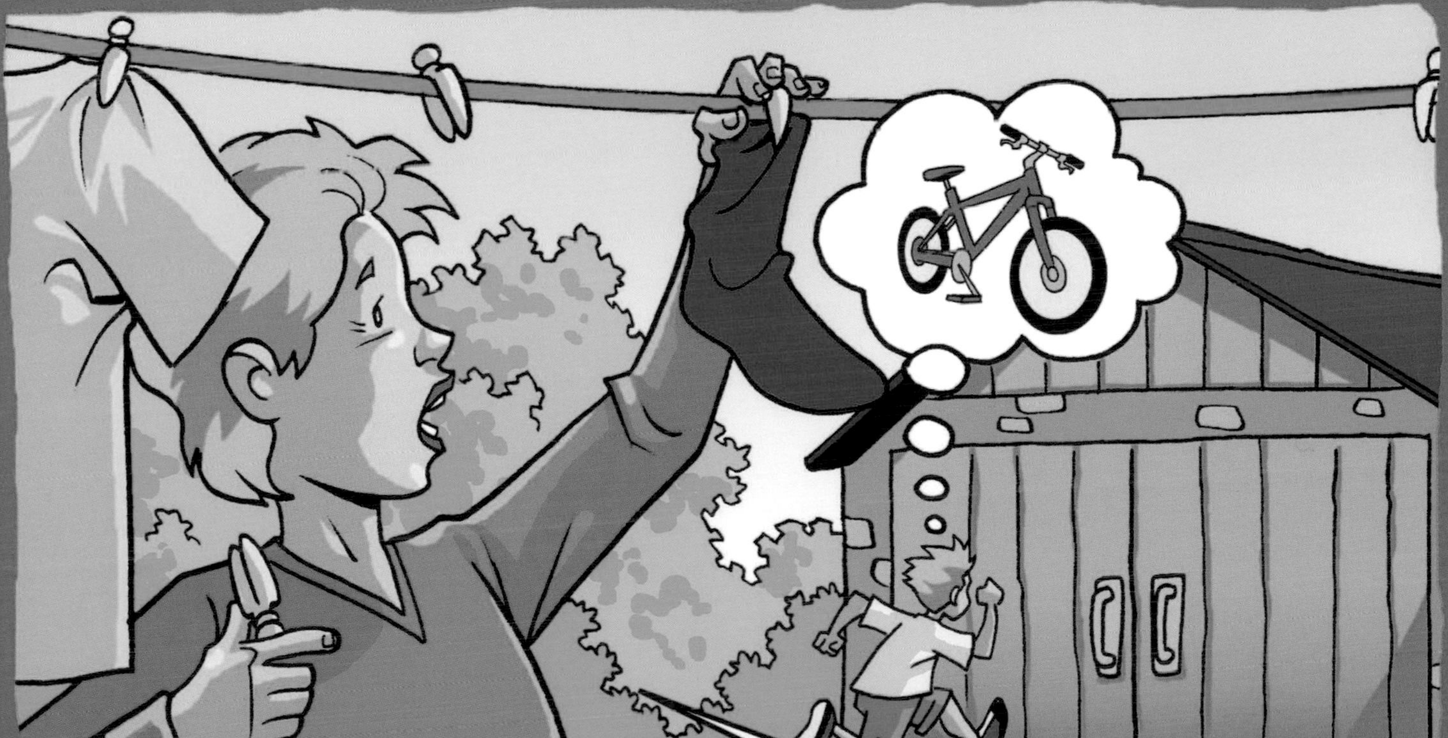
Don't forget Jonnie!

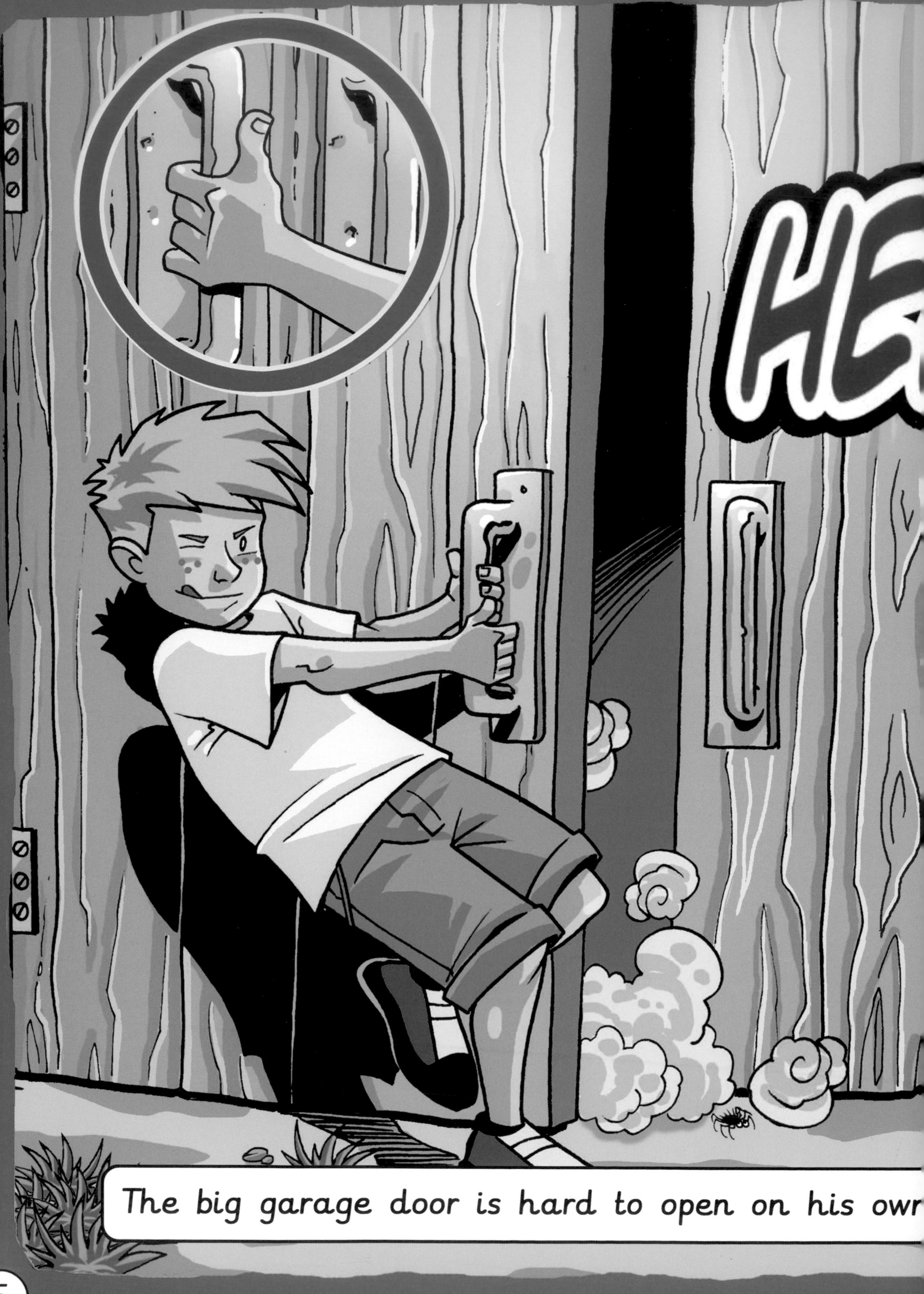
The big garage door is hard to open on his ow

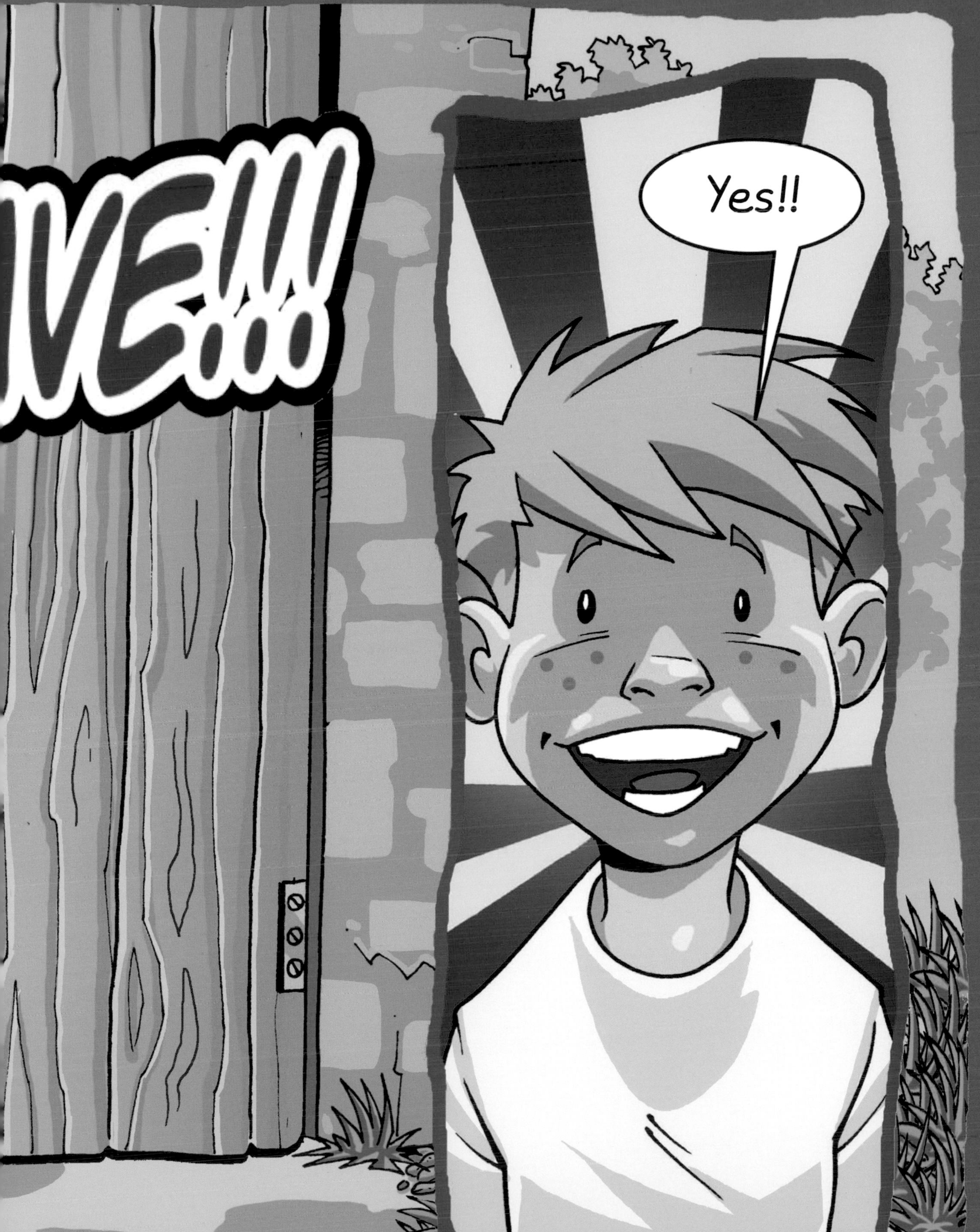
Yes!!

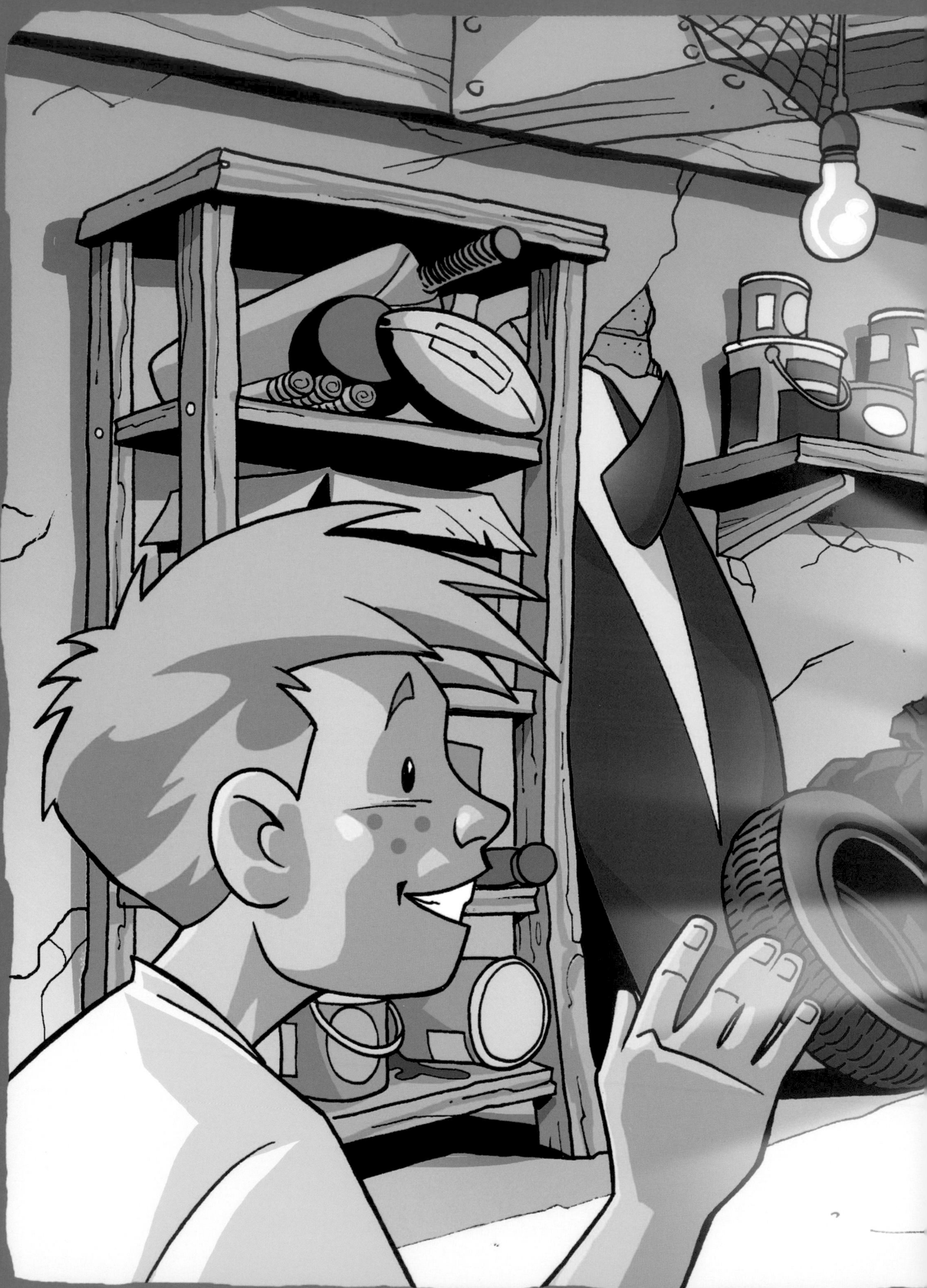

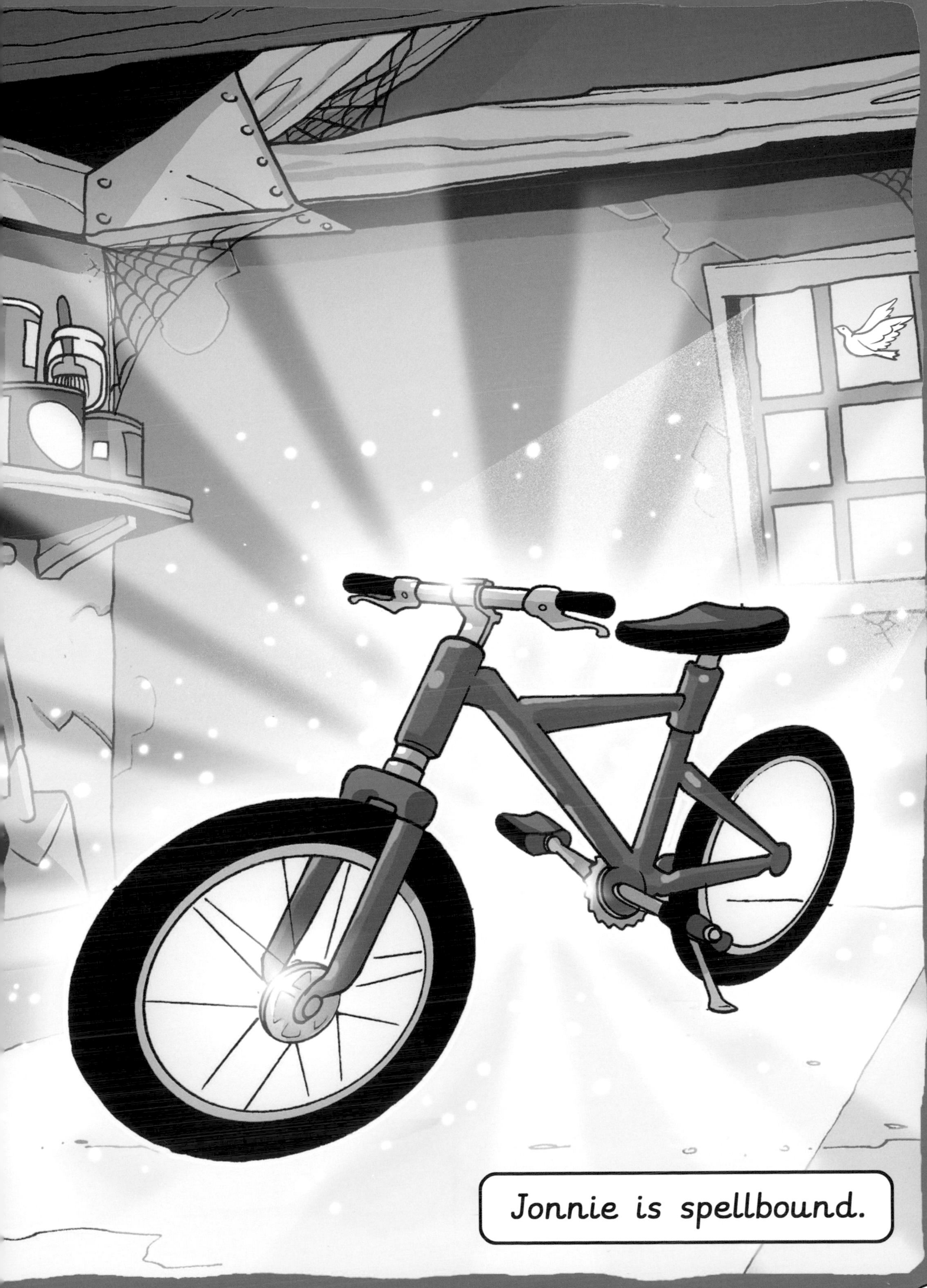
Jonnie is spellbound.

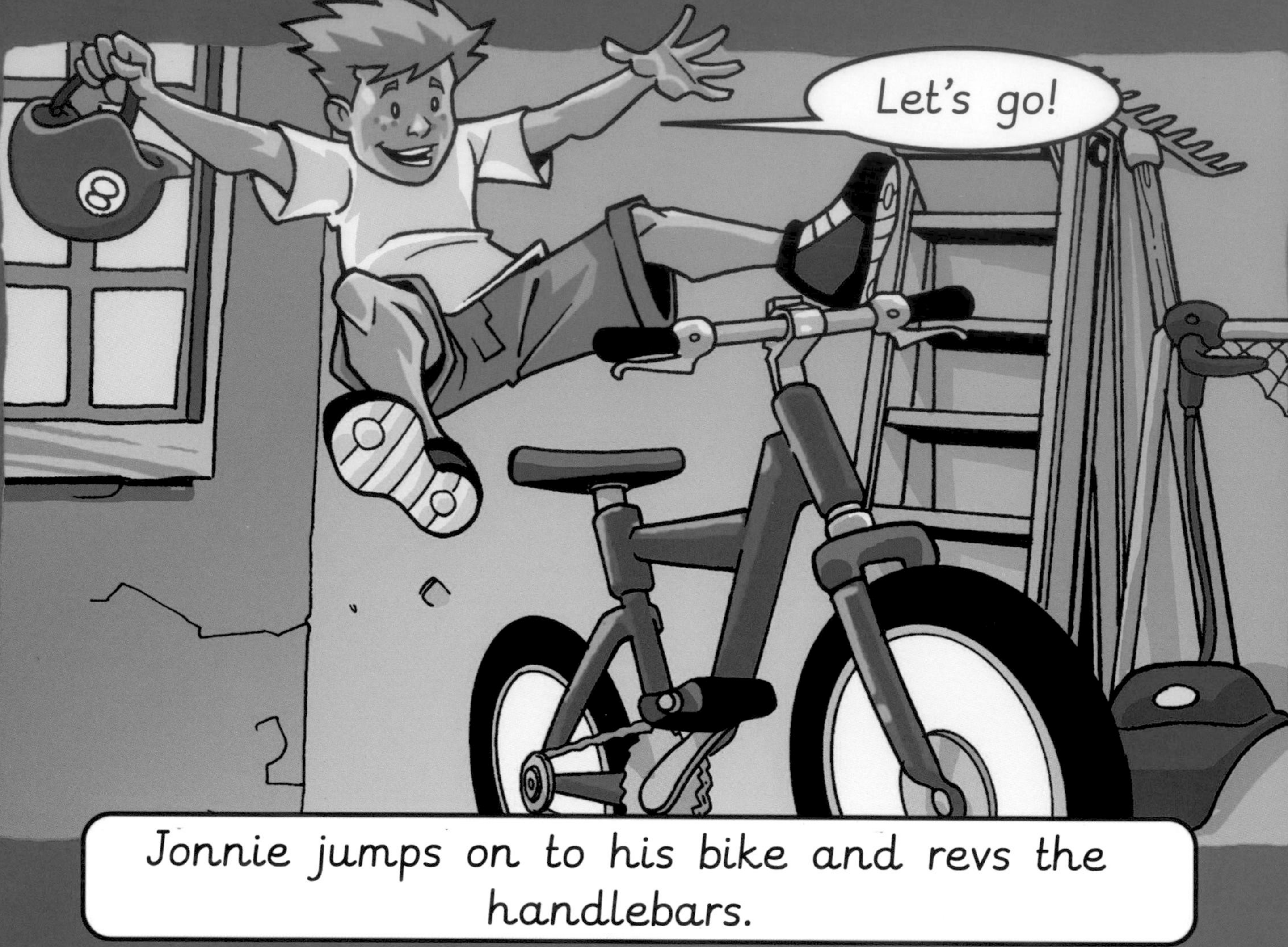
Let's go!
Jonnie jumps on to his bike and revs the handlebars.

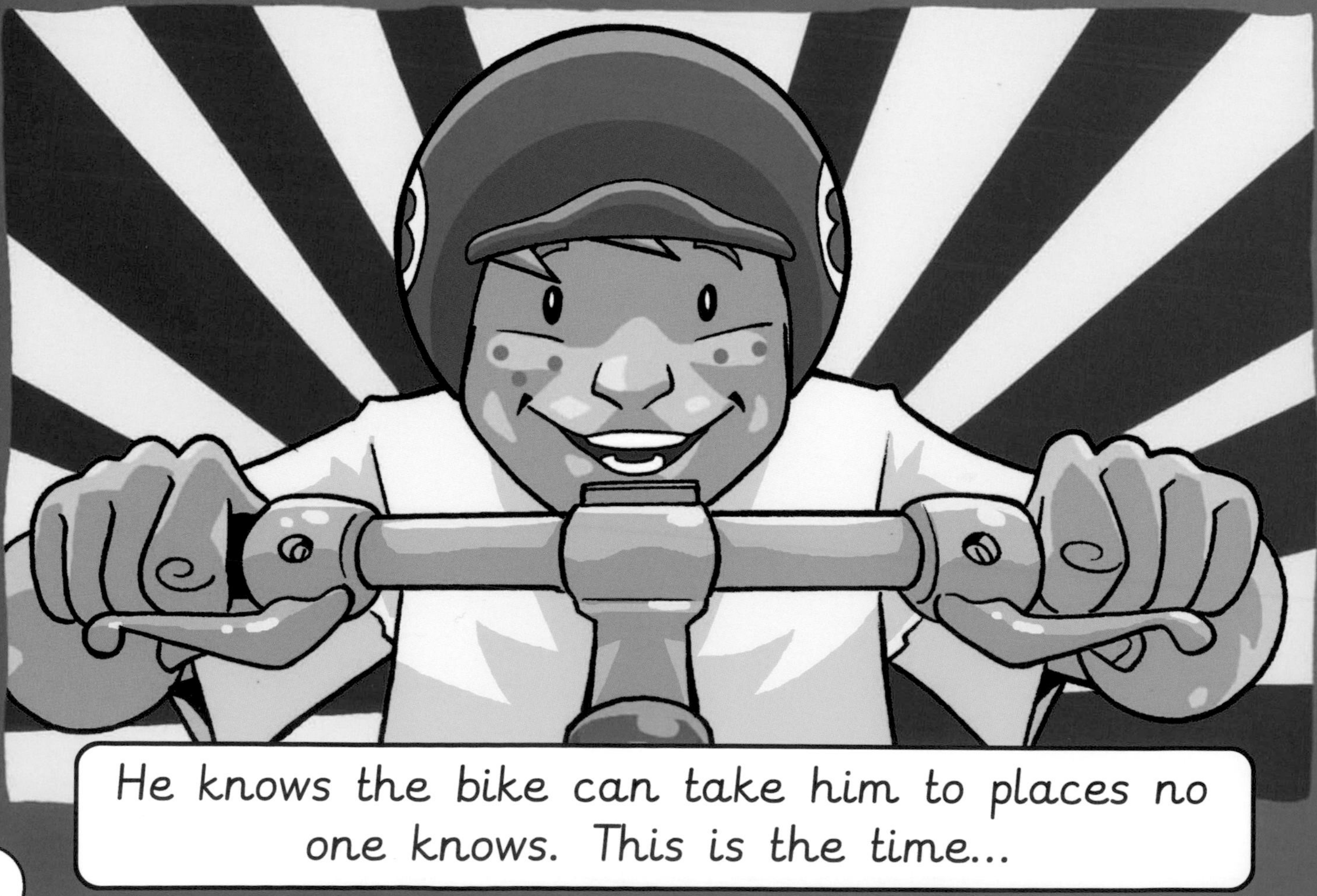
He knows the bike can take him to places no one knows. This is the time...

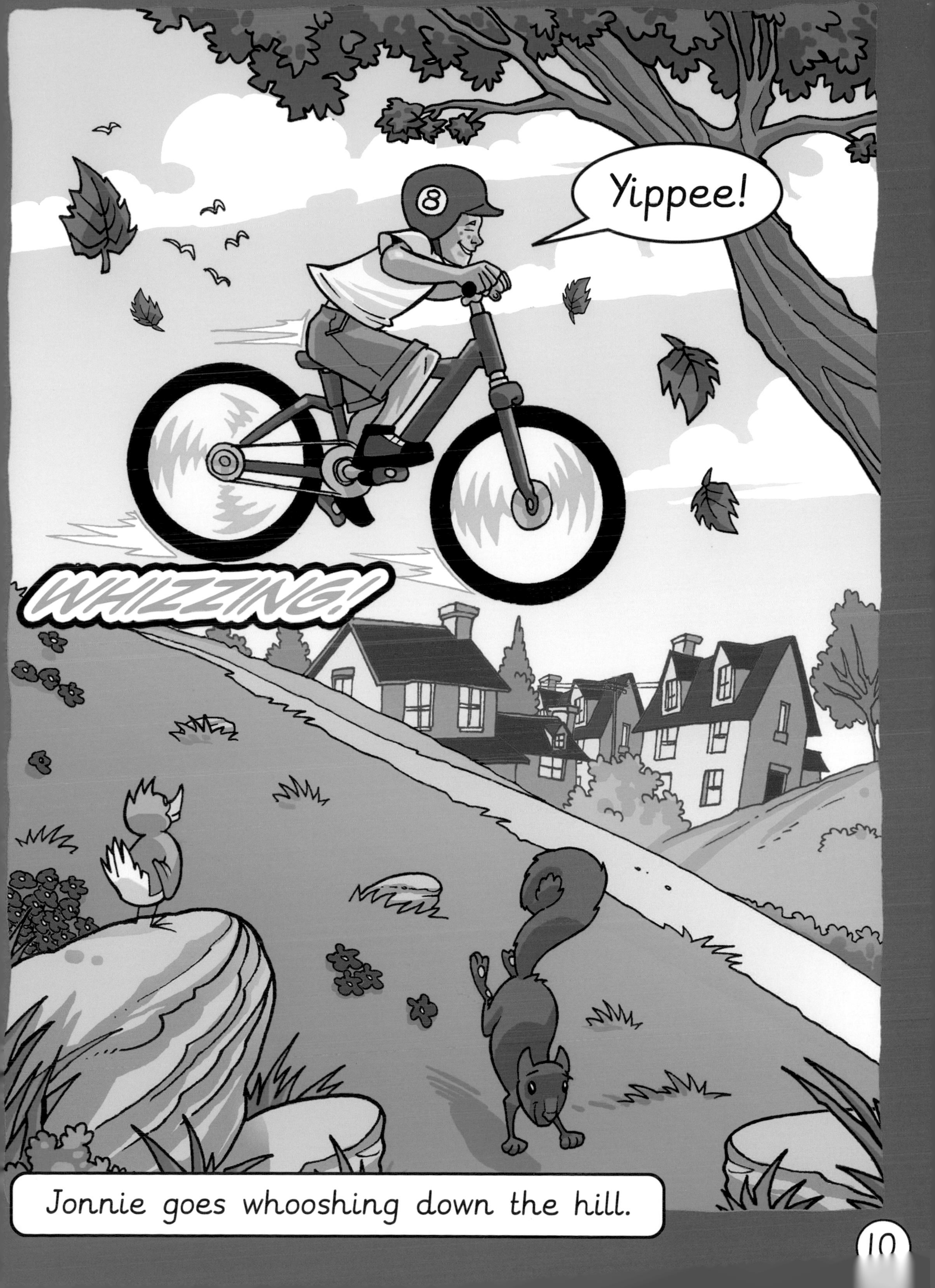
Yippee!
WHIZZING!

Jonnie goes whooshing down the hill.

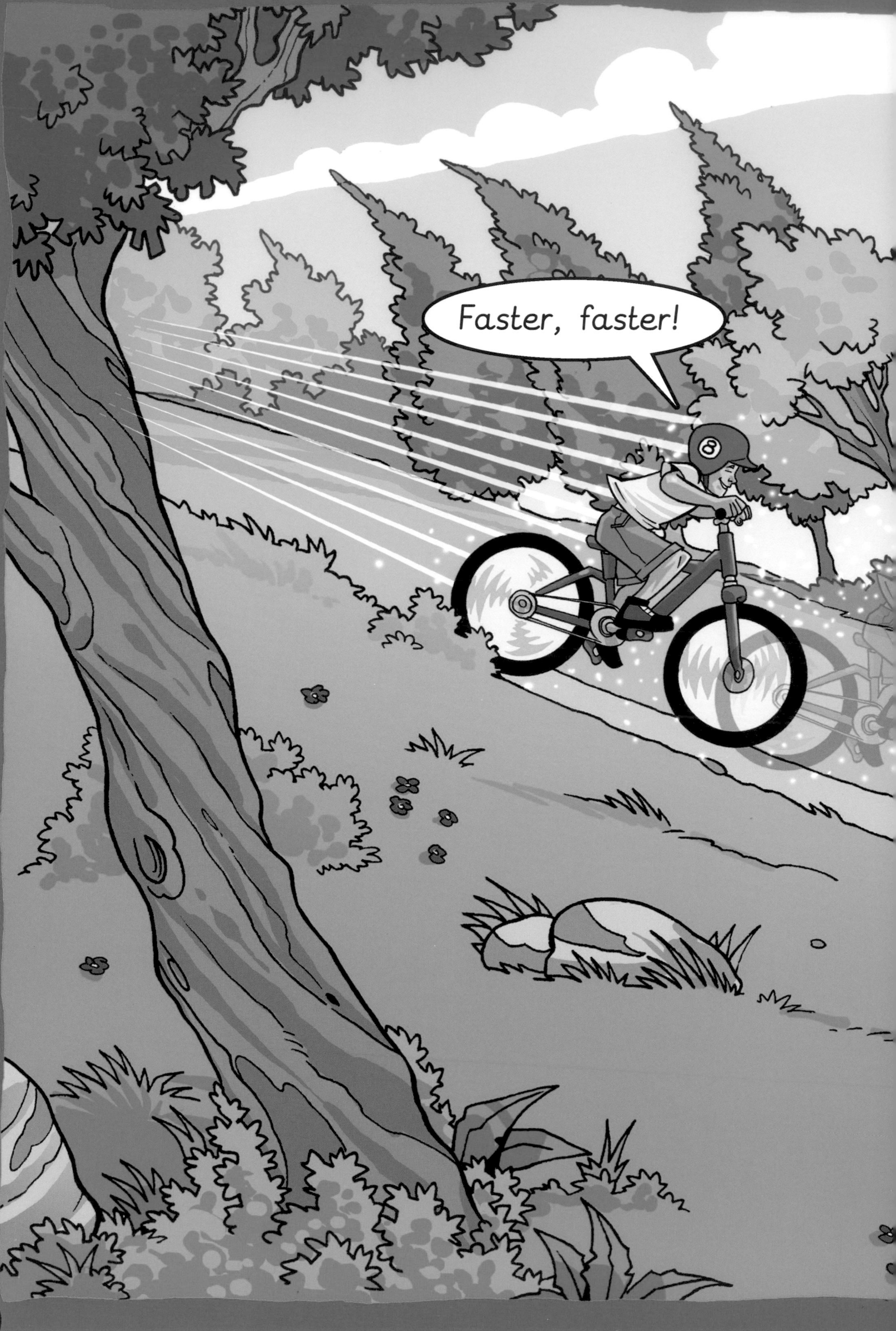
Faster, faster!

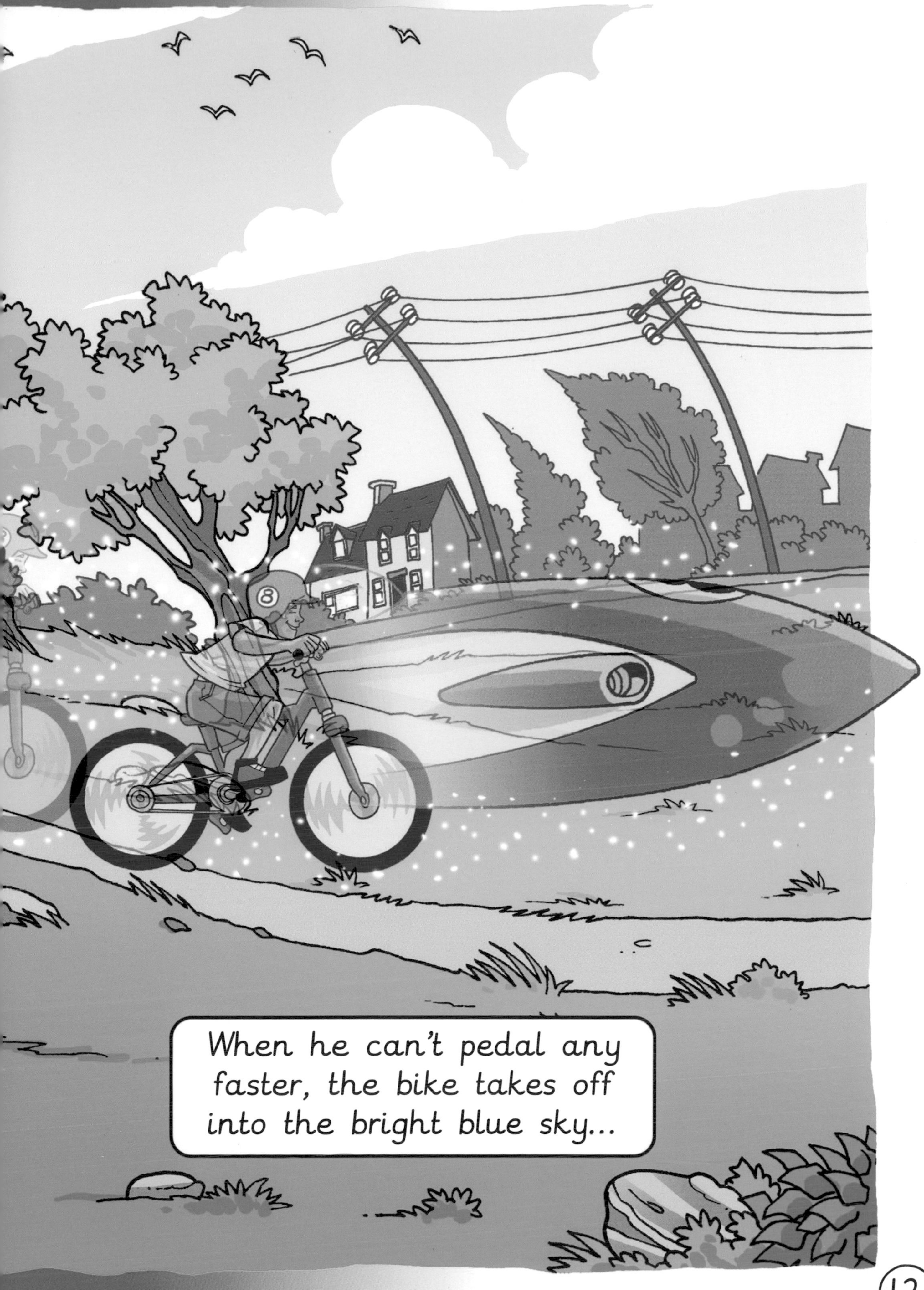
When he can't pedal any faster, the bike takes off into the bright blue sky...

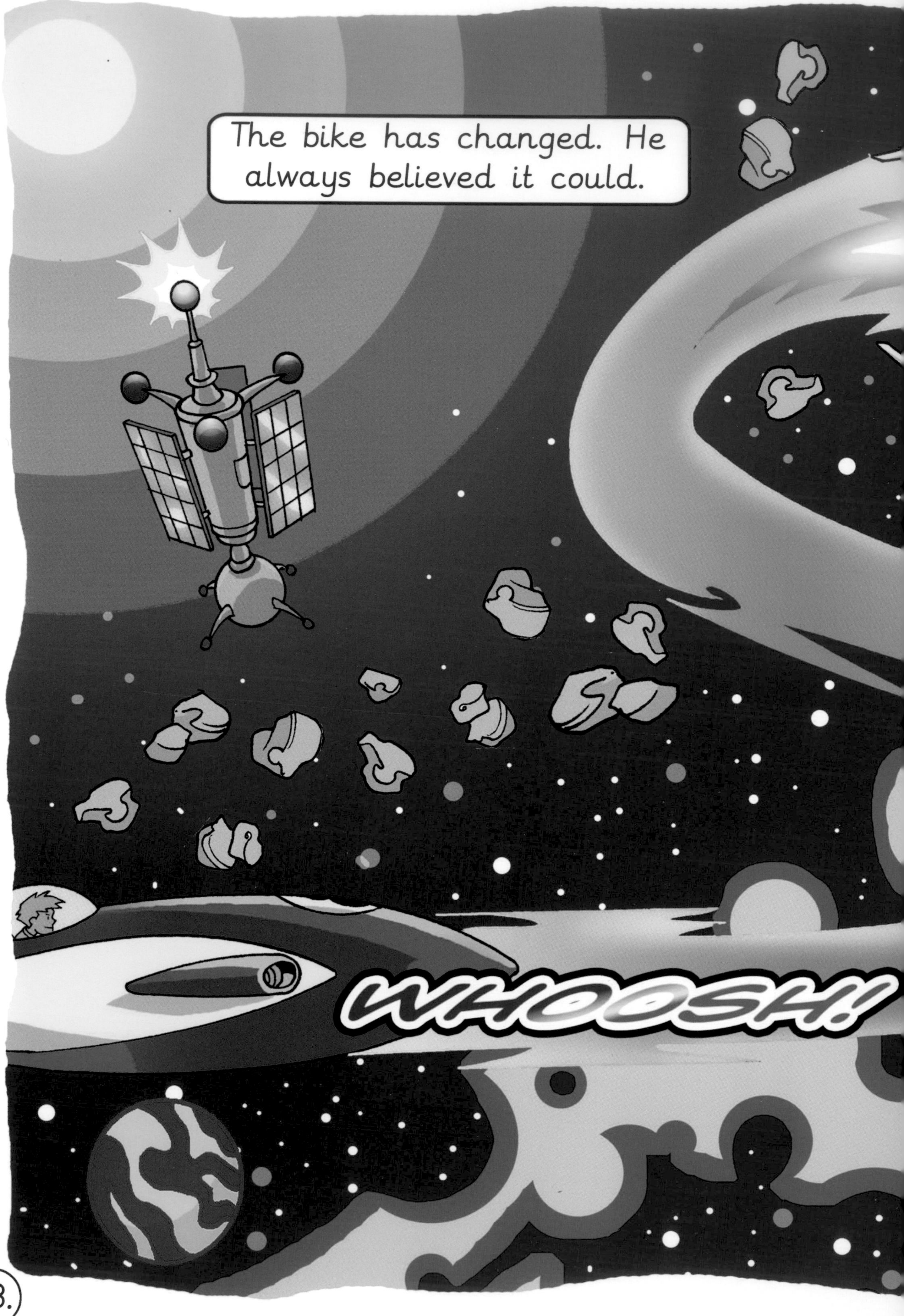
The bike has changed. He always believed it could.
WHOOSH!

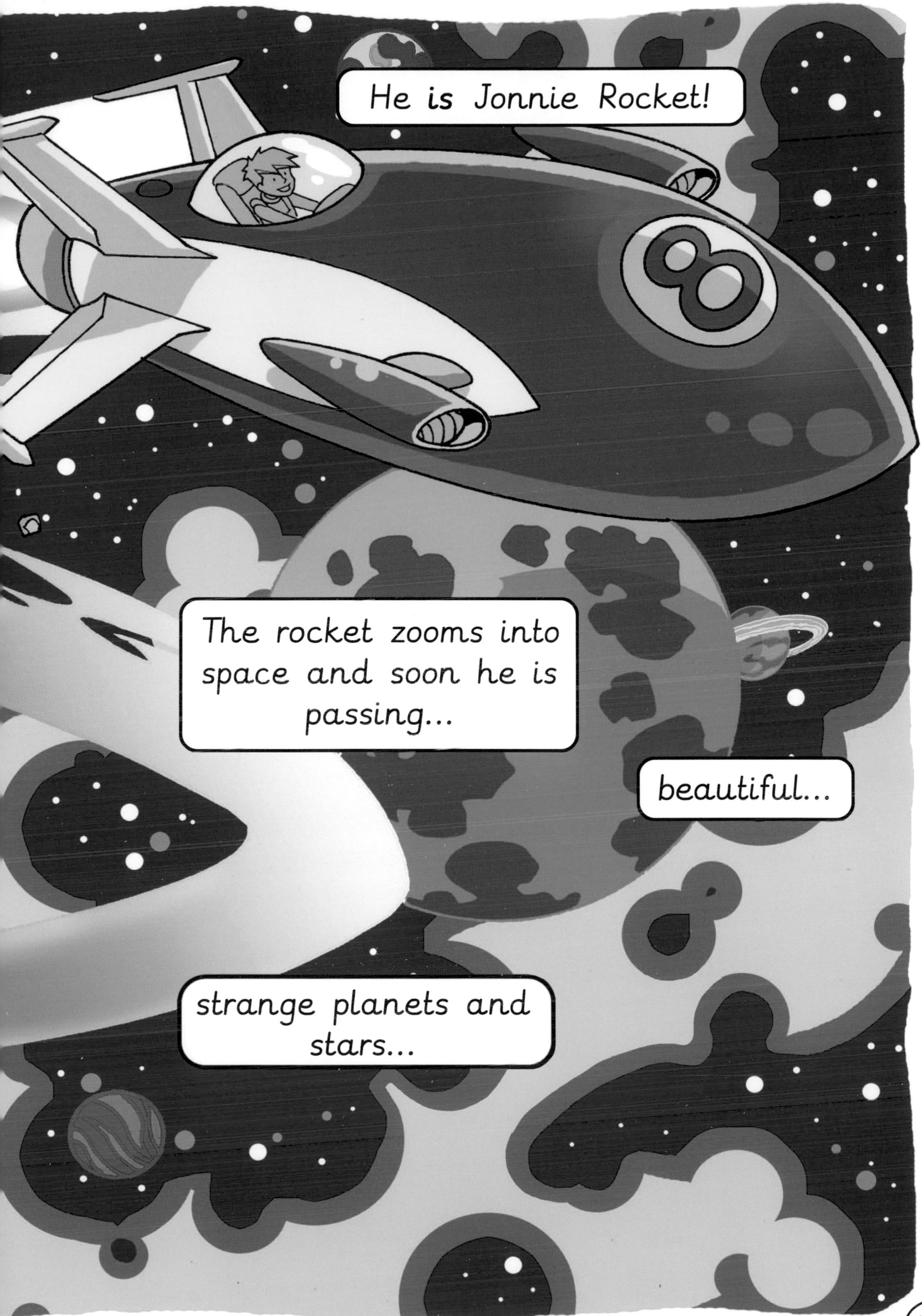
He is Jonnie Rocket!
The rocket zooms into space and soon he is passing...
beautiful...
strange planets and stars...

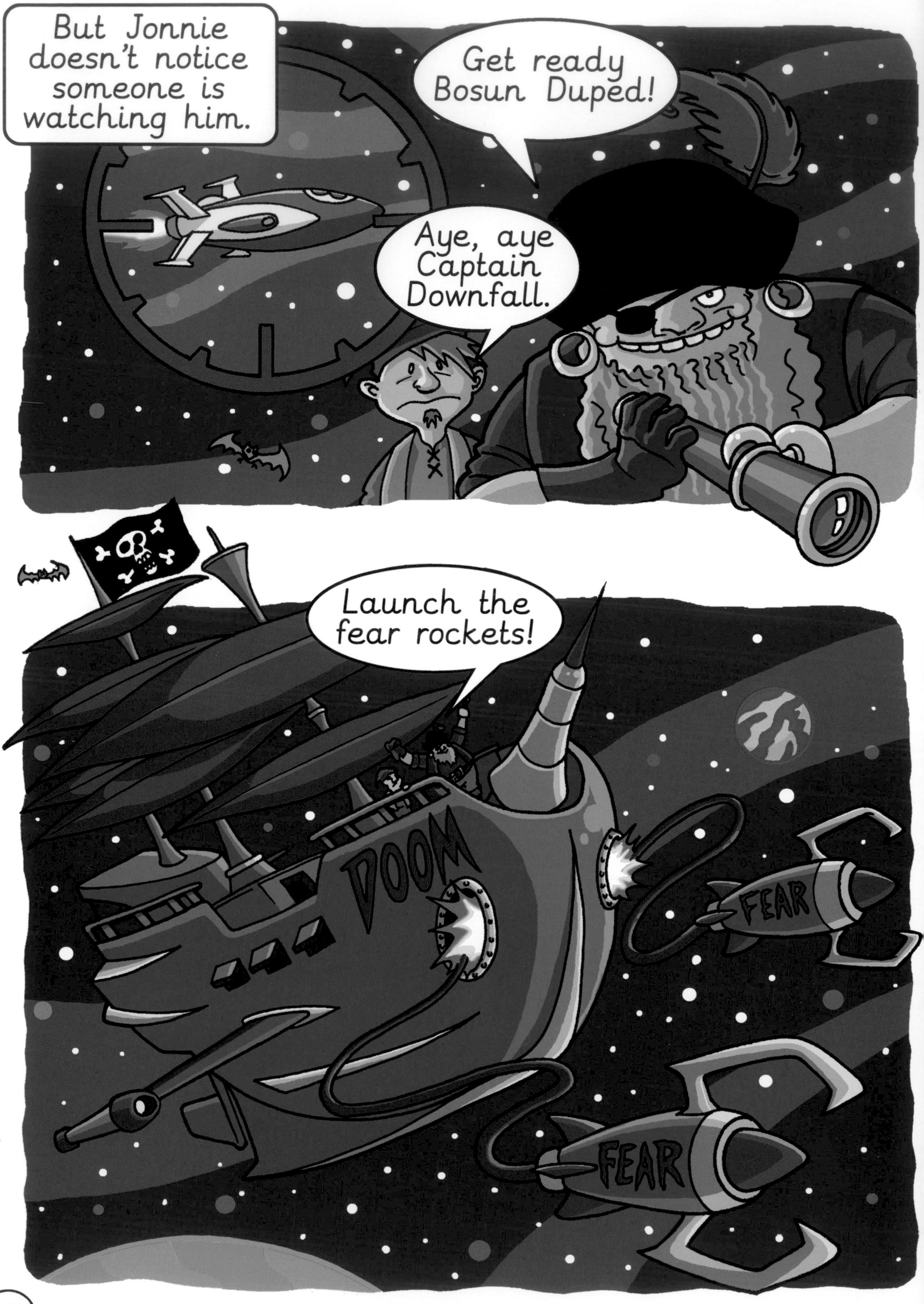
But Jonnie doesn't notice someone is watching him.
Get ready Bosun Duped!
Aye, aye Captain Downfall.
Launch the fear rockets!
DOOM
FEAR
FEAR

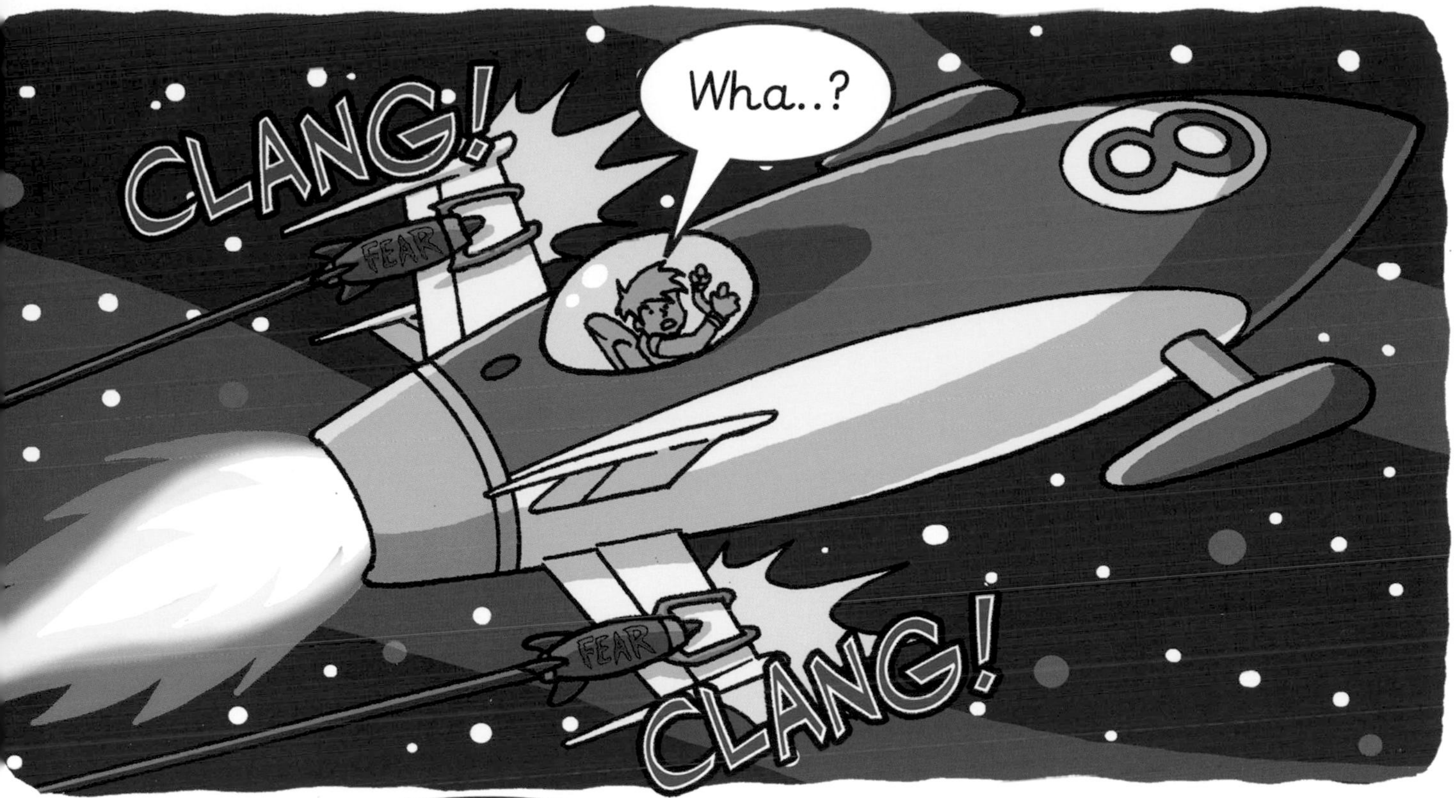
CLANG!
Wha..?
FEAR
FEAR
CLANG!

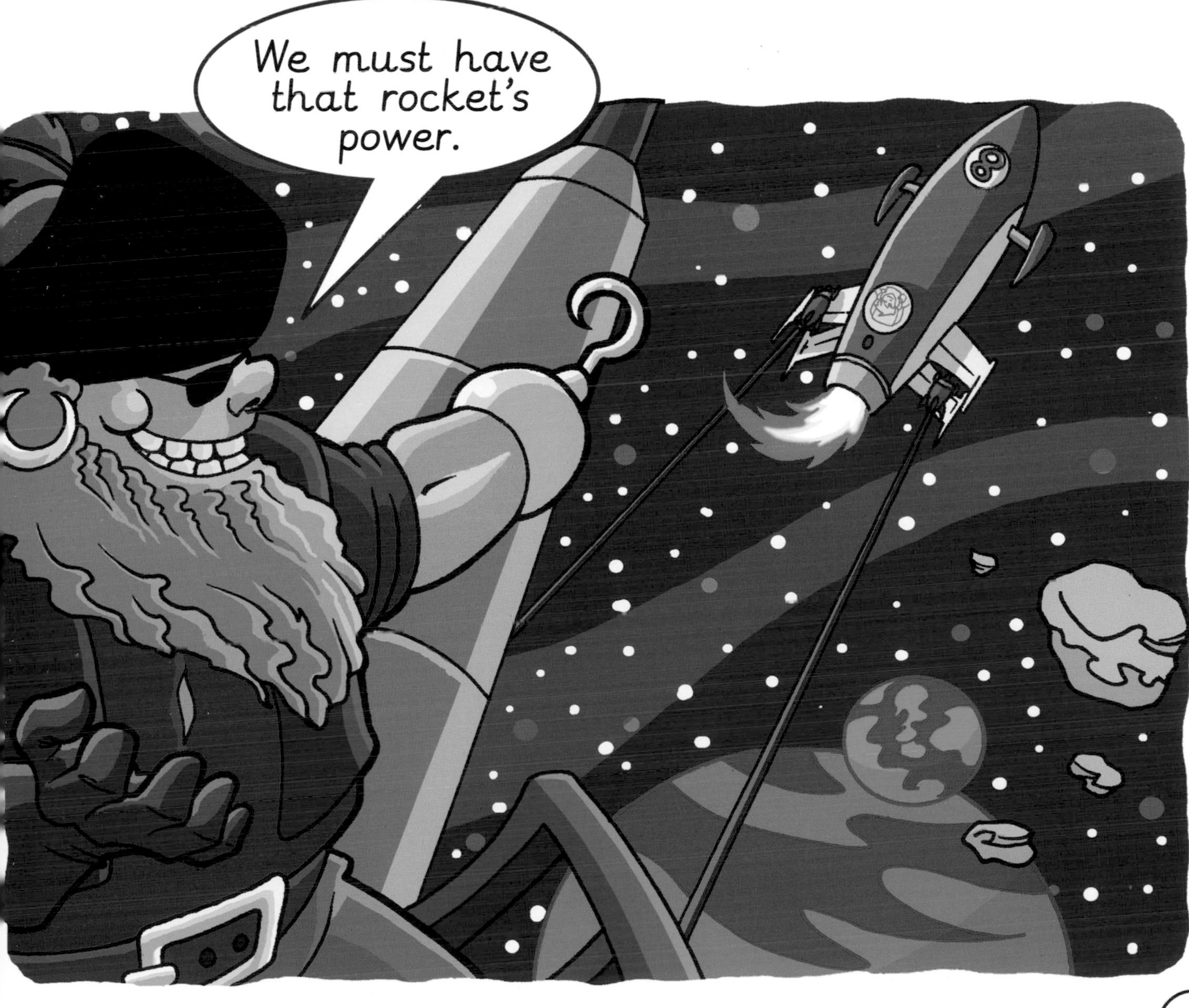
We must have that rocket's power.

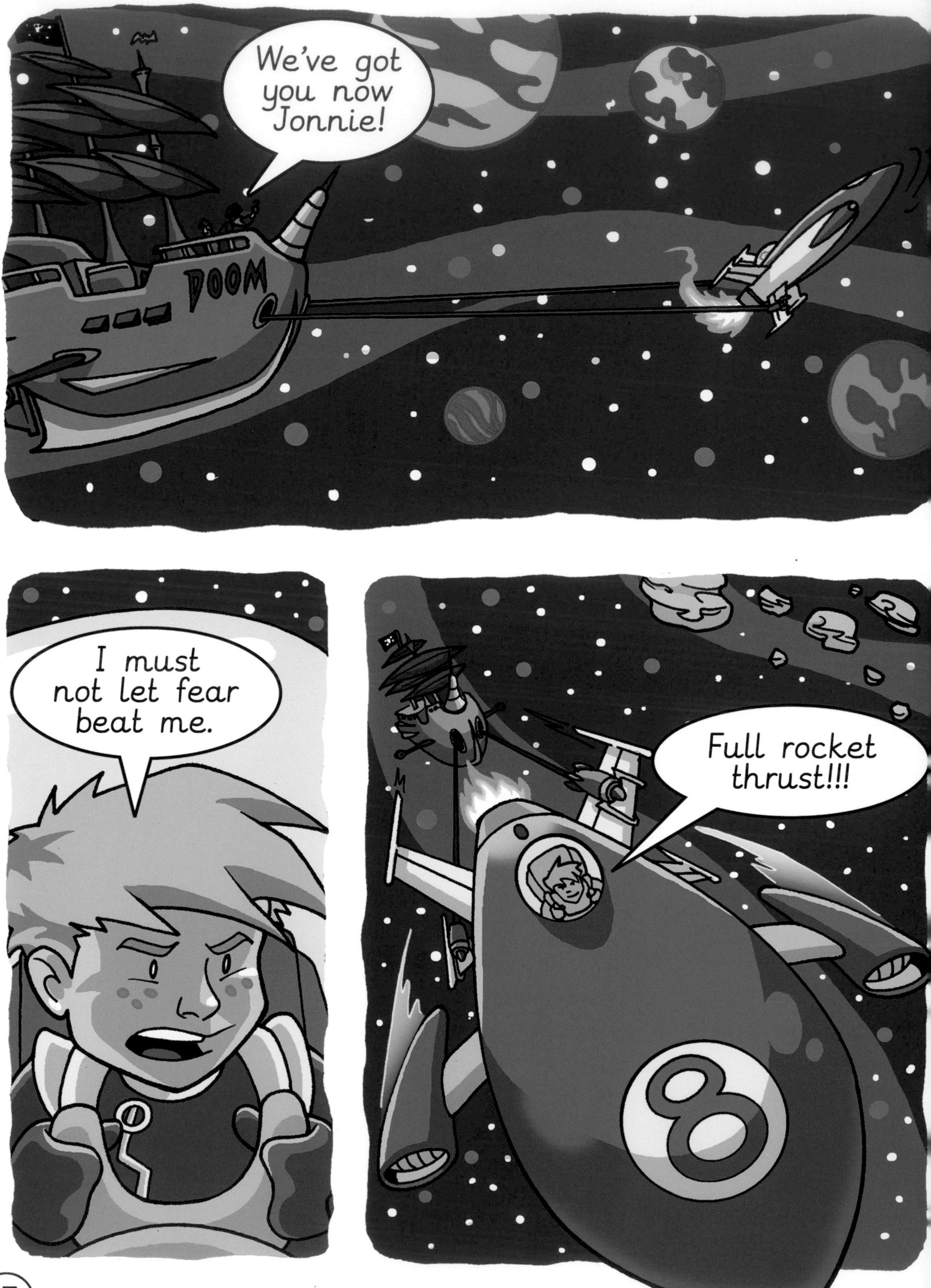
We've got you now Jonnie!
DOOM
I must not let fear beat me.
Full rocket thrust!!!

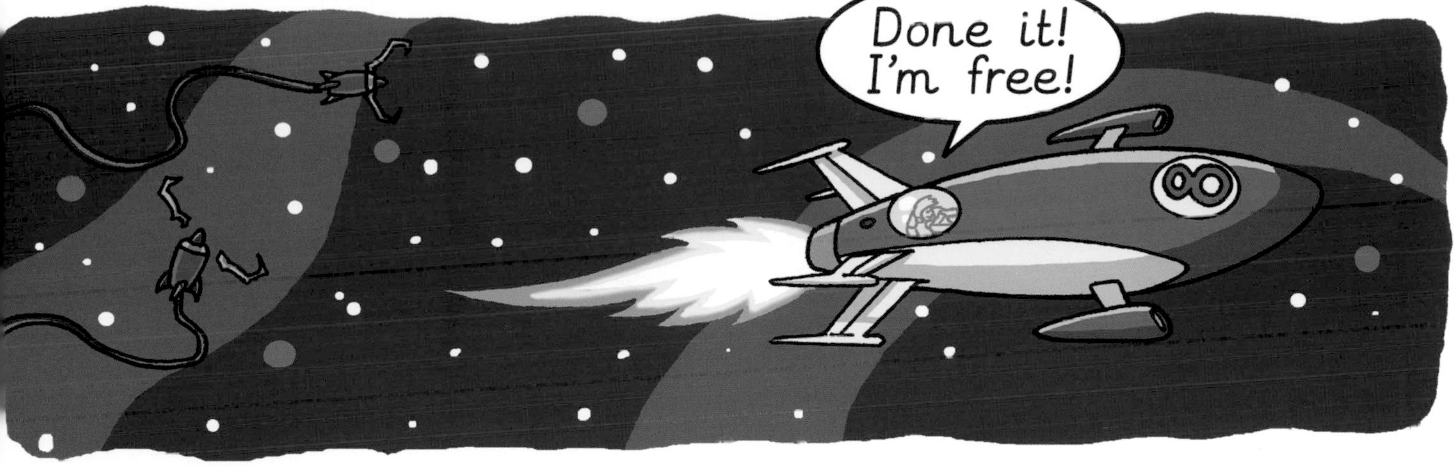
Done it! I'm free!

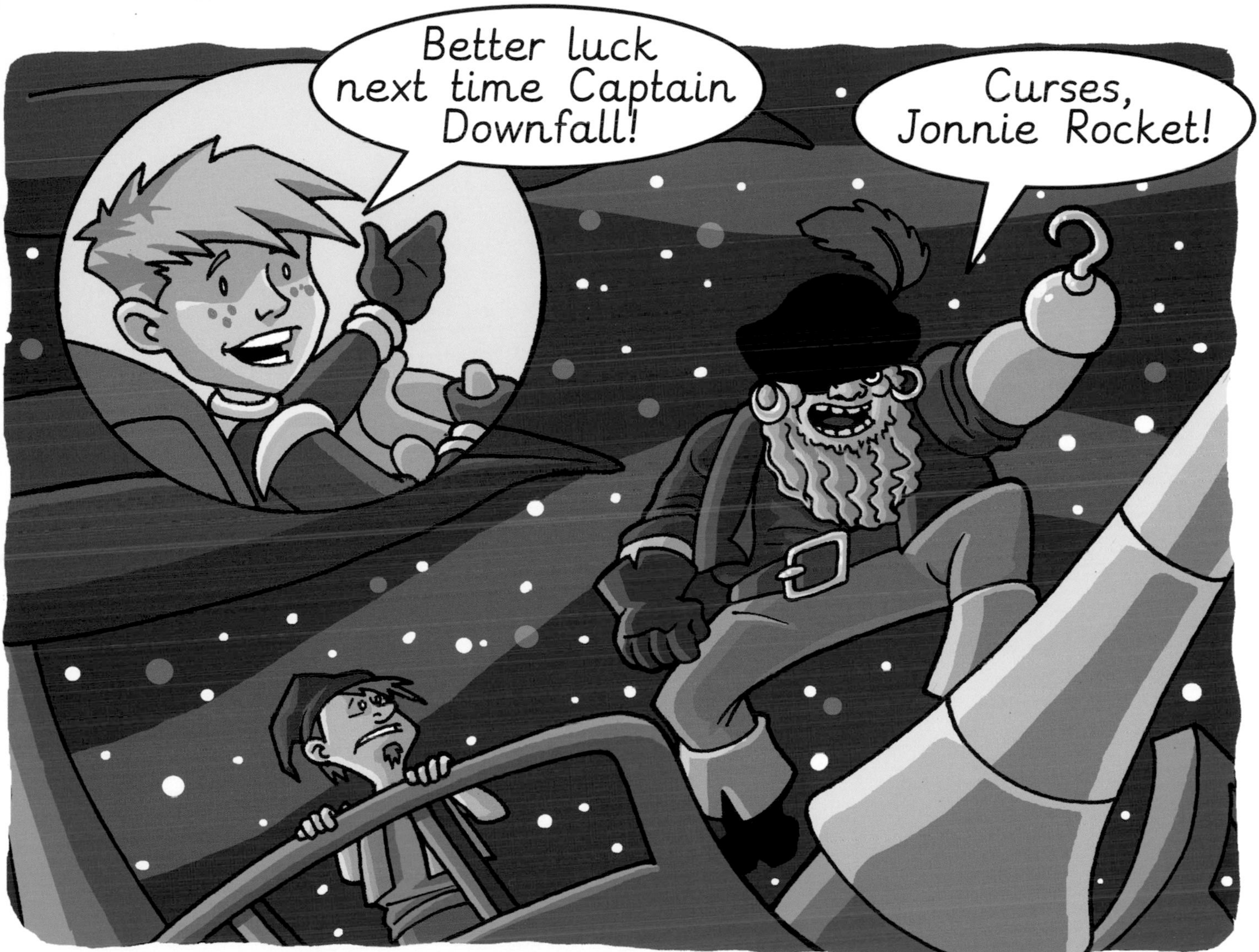
Better luck next time Captain Downfall!
Curses, Jonnie Rocket!

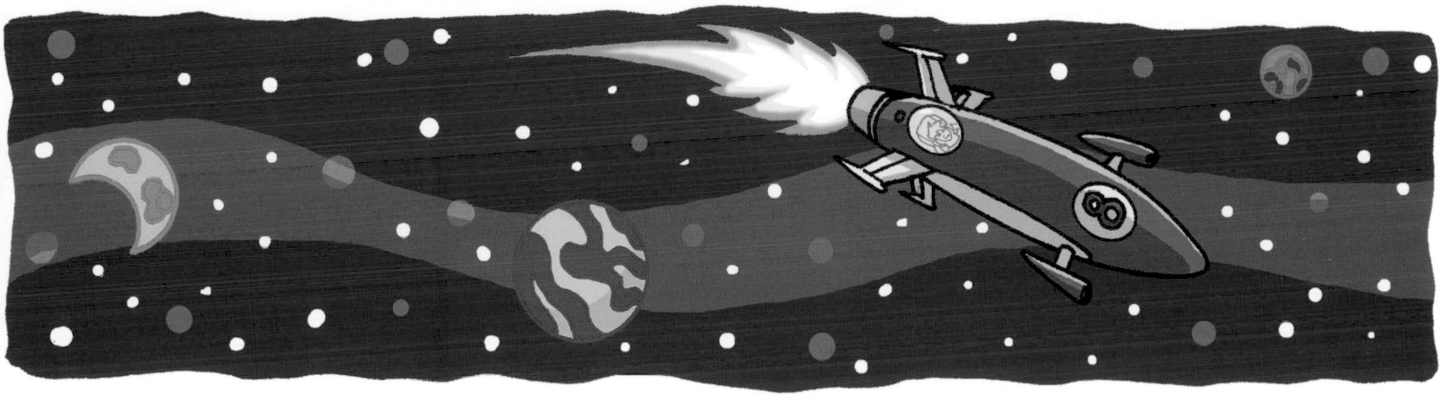

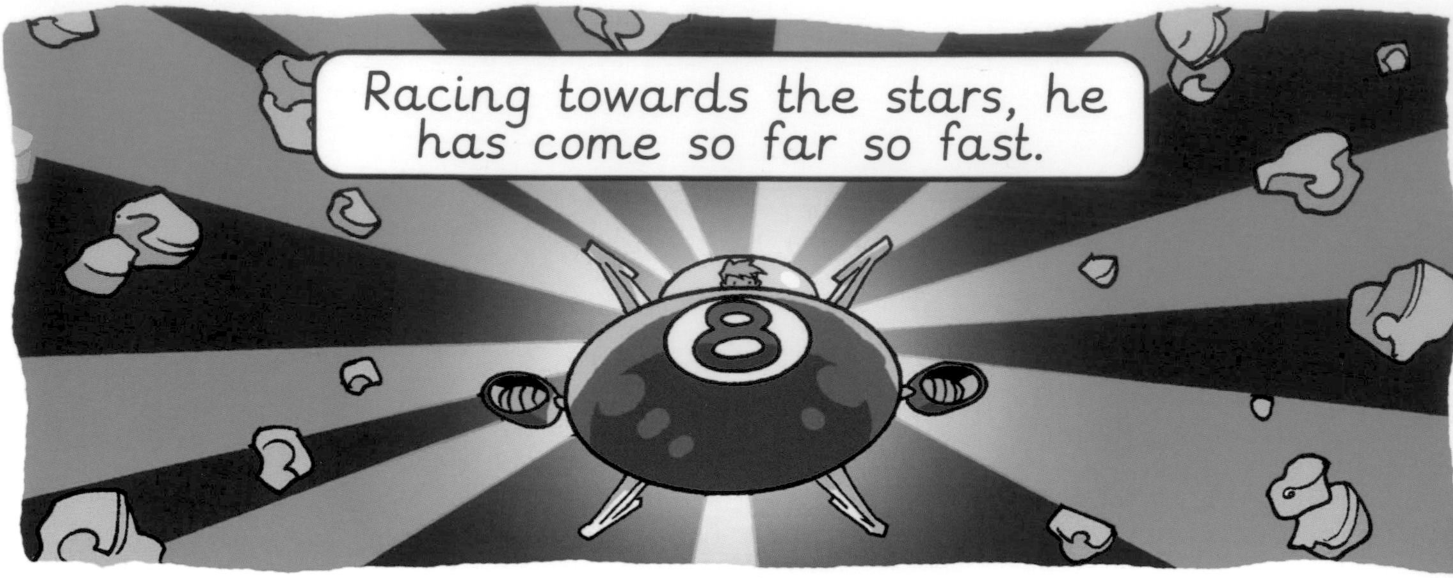
Racing towards the stars, he has come so far so fast.

Far above the stars, the planet Earth is blue.

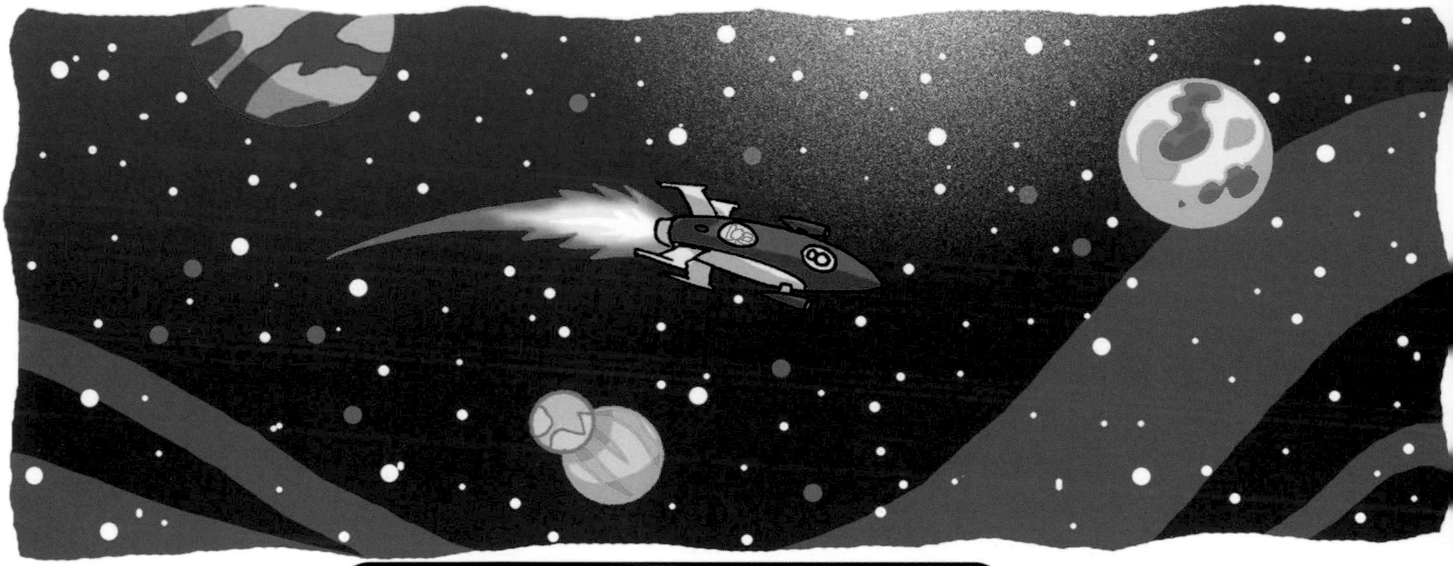

The space ship knows which way to go.

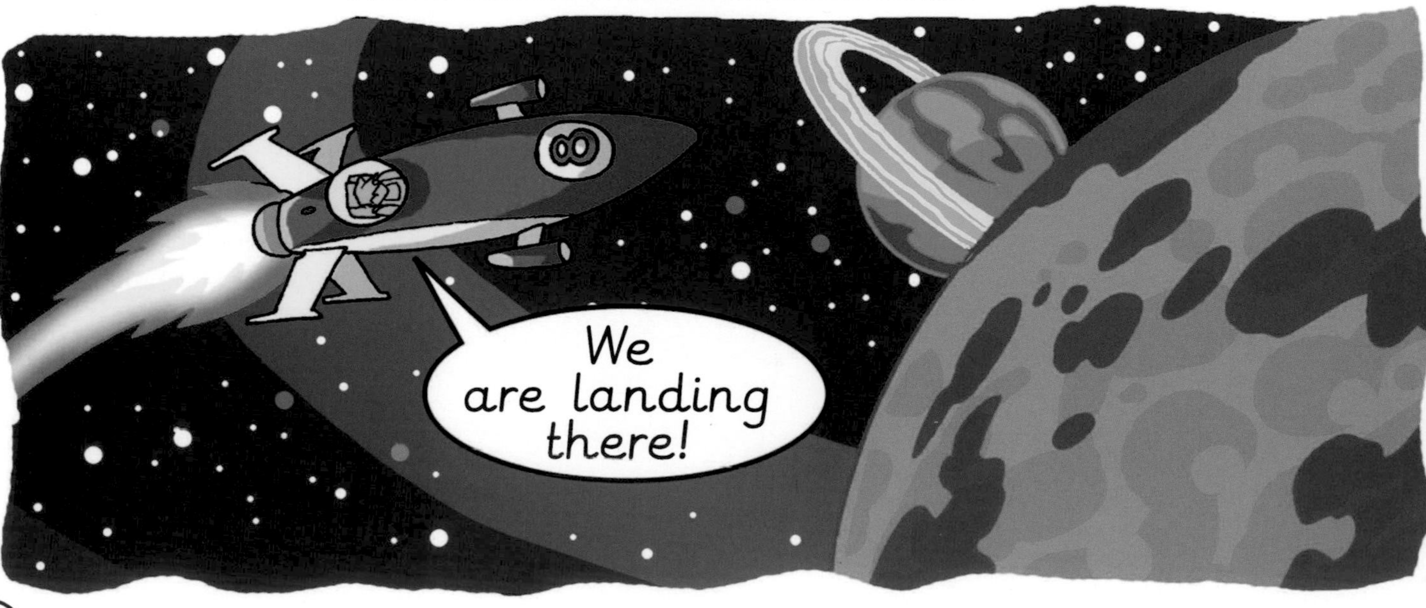
We are landing there!

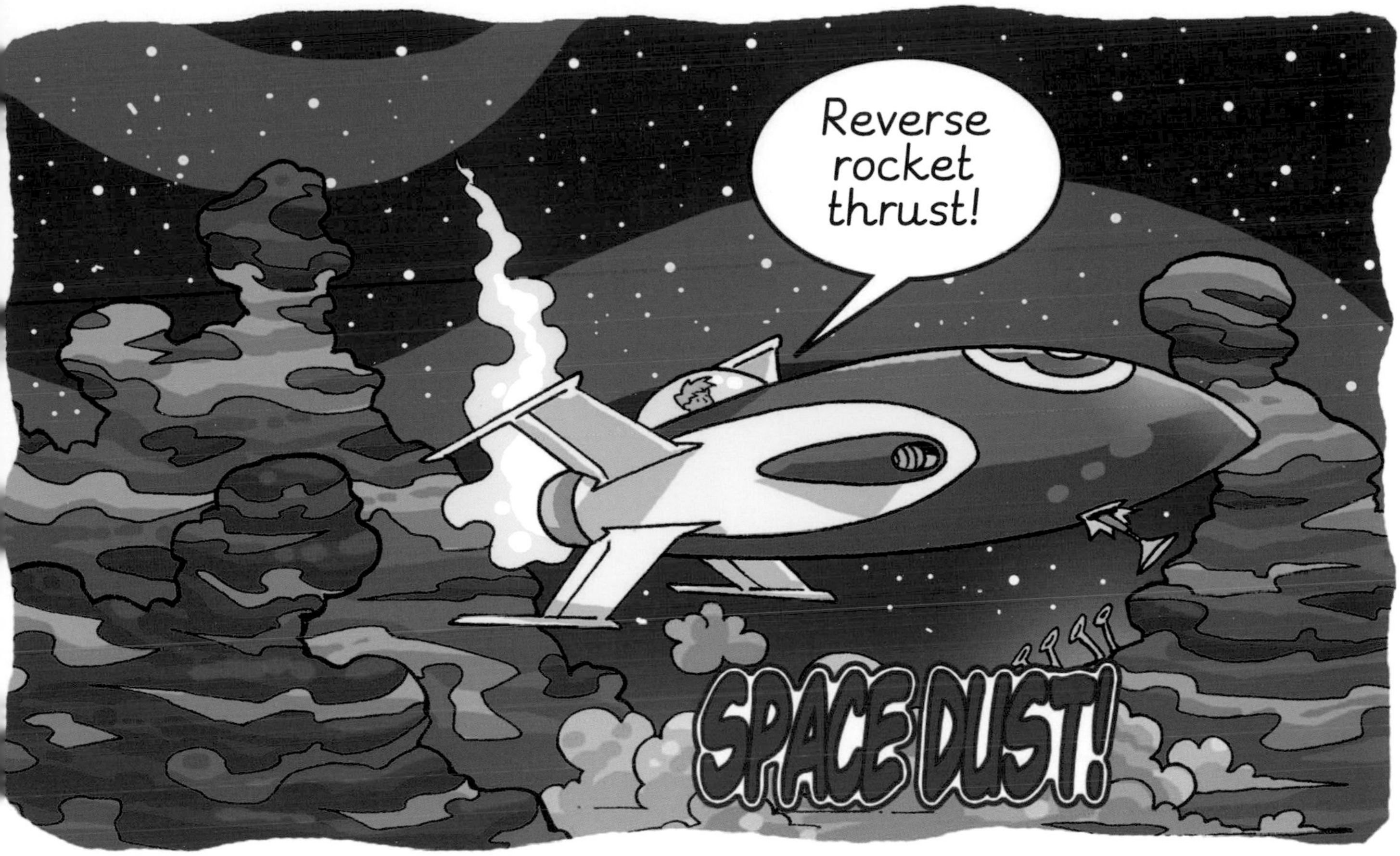
Reverse rocket thrust!
SPACE DUST!

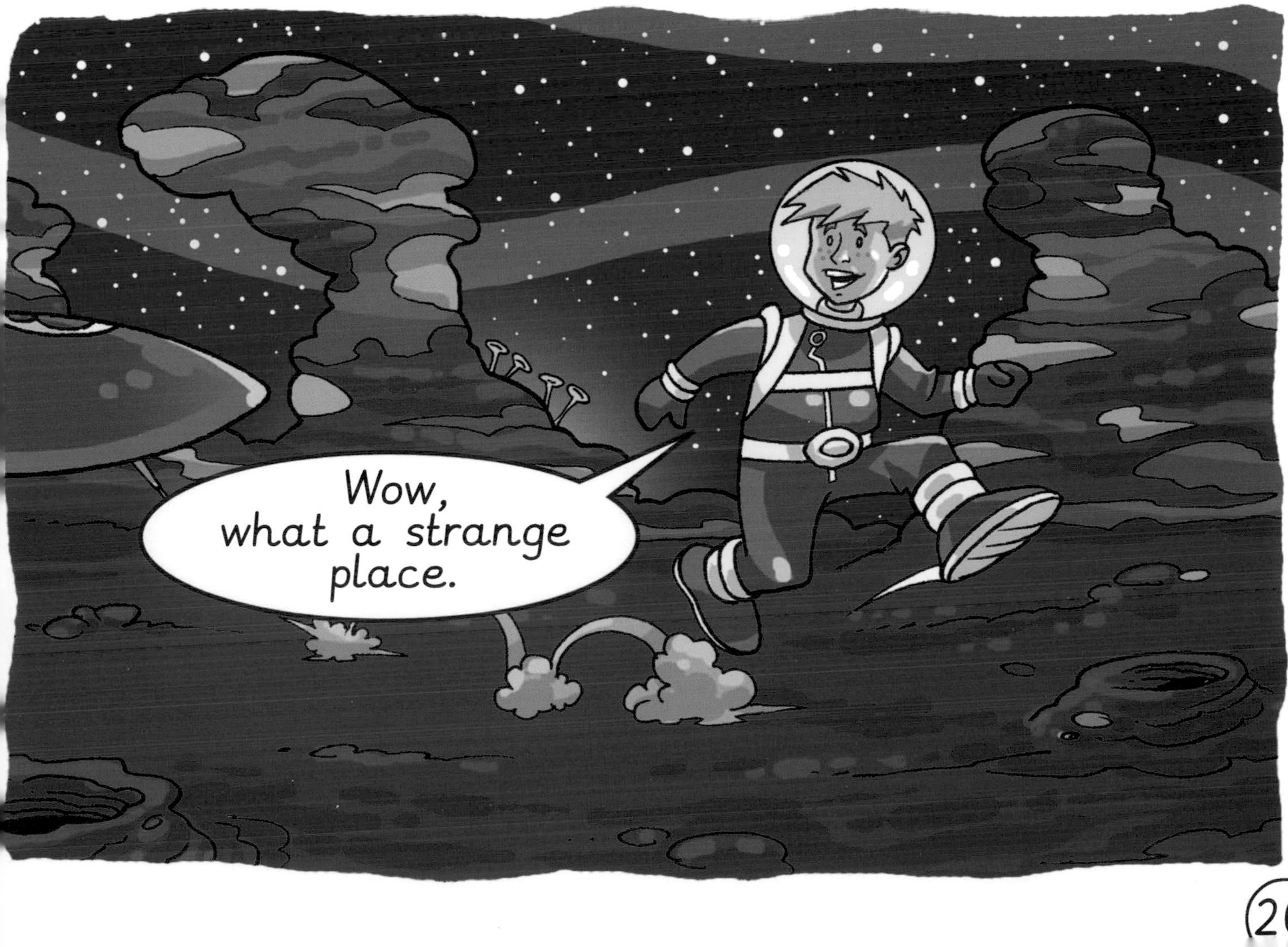
Wow, what a strange place.

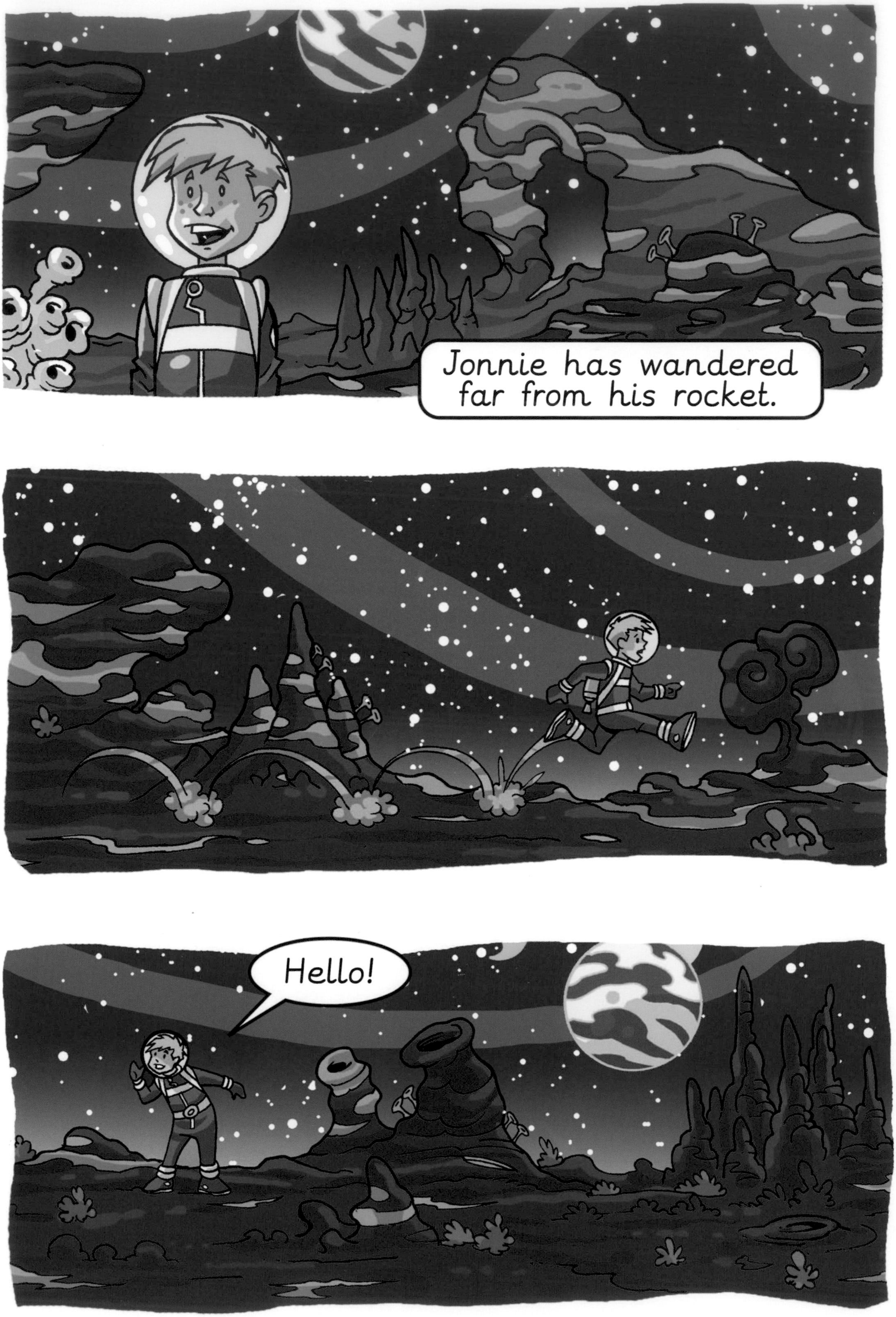
Jonnie has wandered far from his rocket.
Hello!

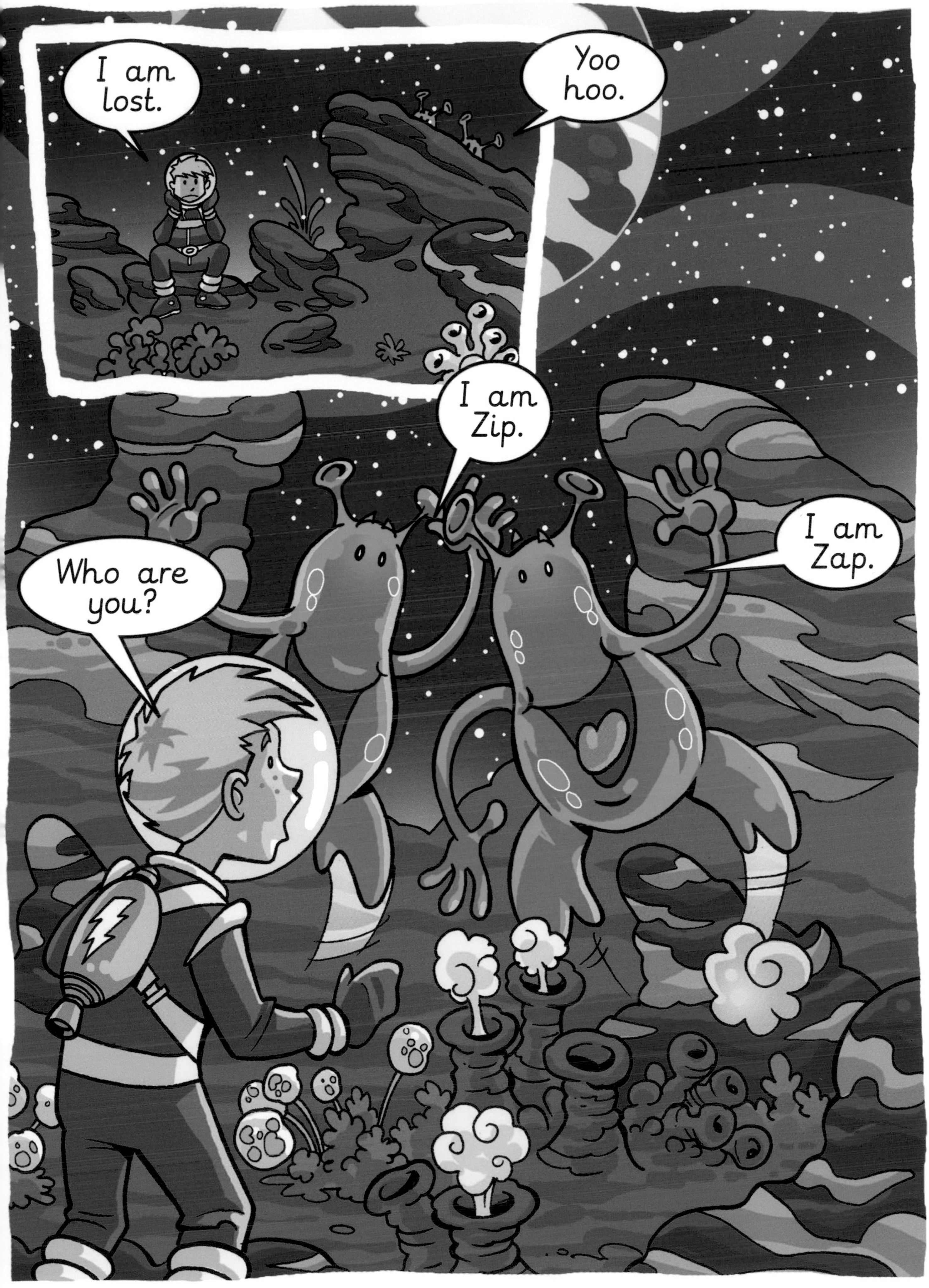
I am lost.
Yoo hoo.
Who are you?
I am Zip.
I am Zap.

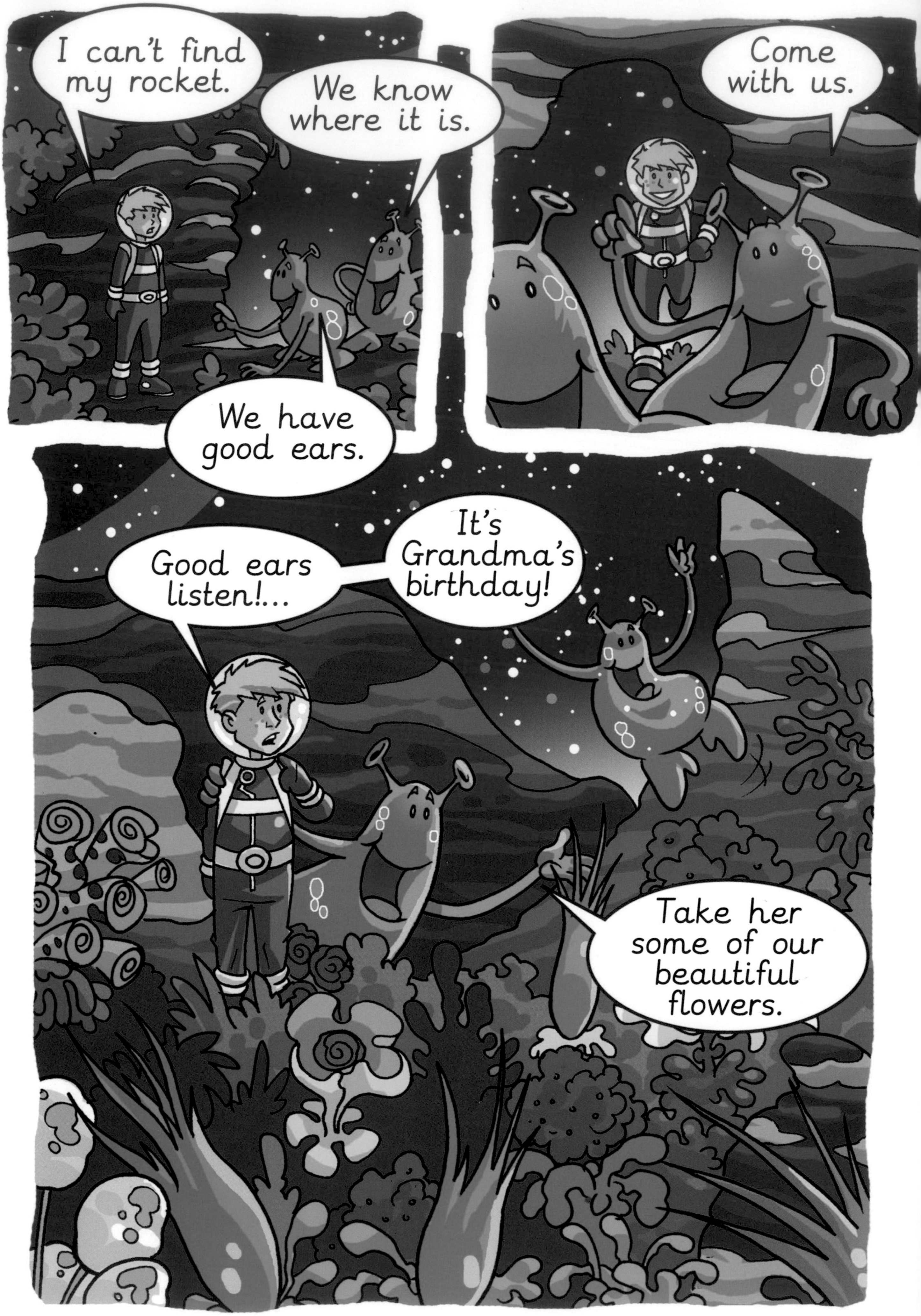
I can't find my rocket.
We know where it is.
We have good ears.
Come with us.
Good ears listen!...
It's Grandma's birthday!
Take her some of our beautiful flowers.

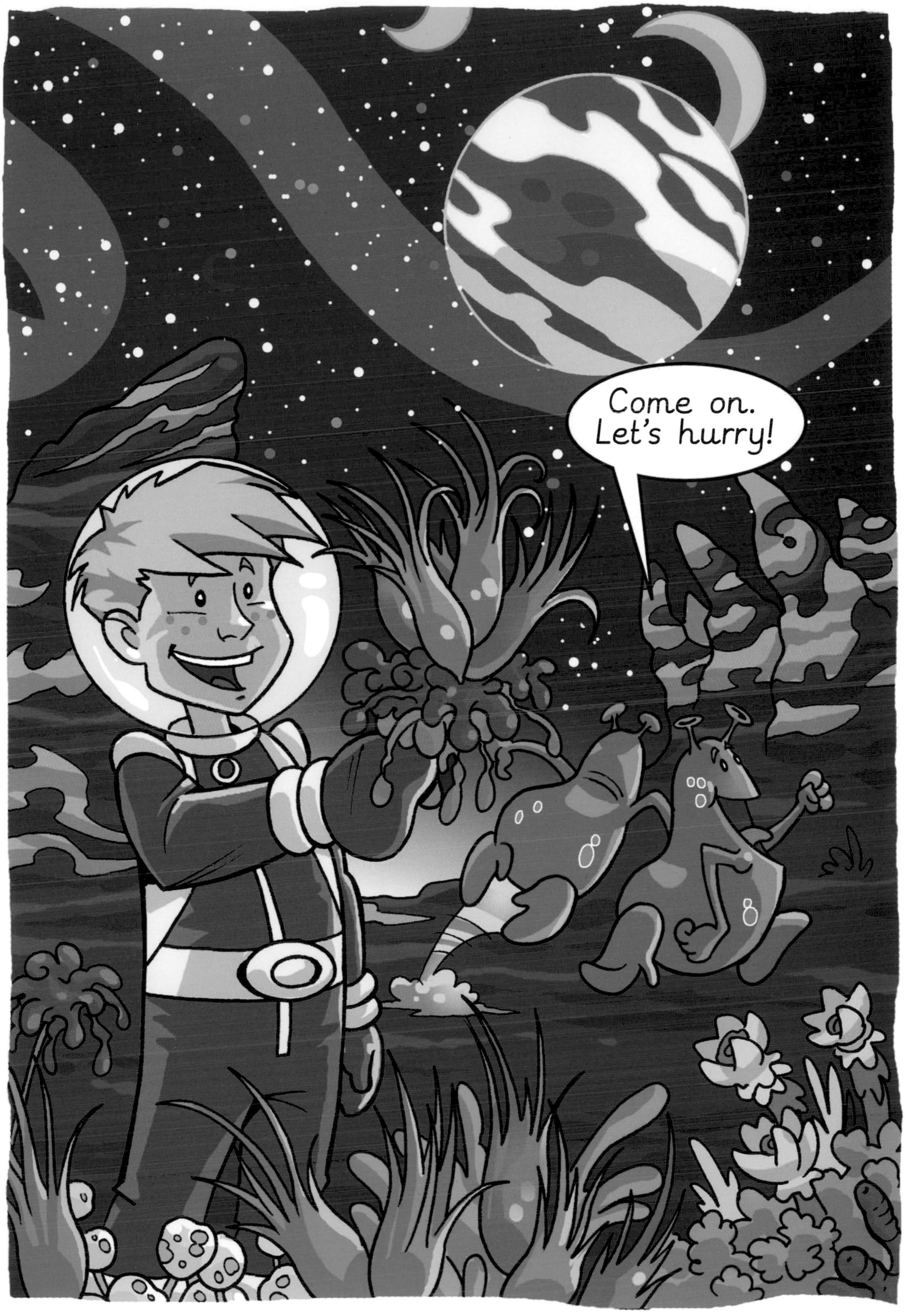
Come on. Let's hurry!

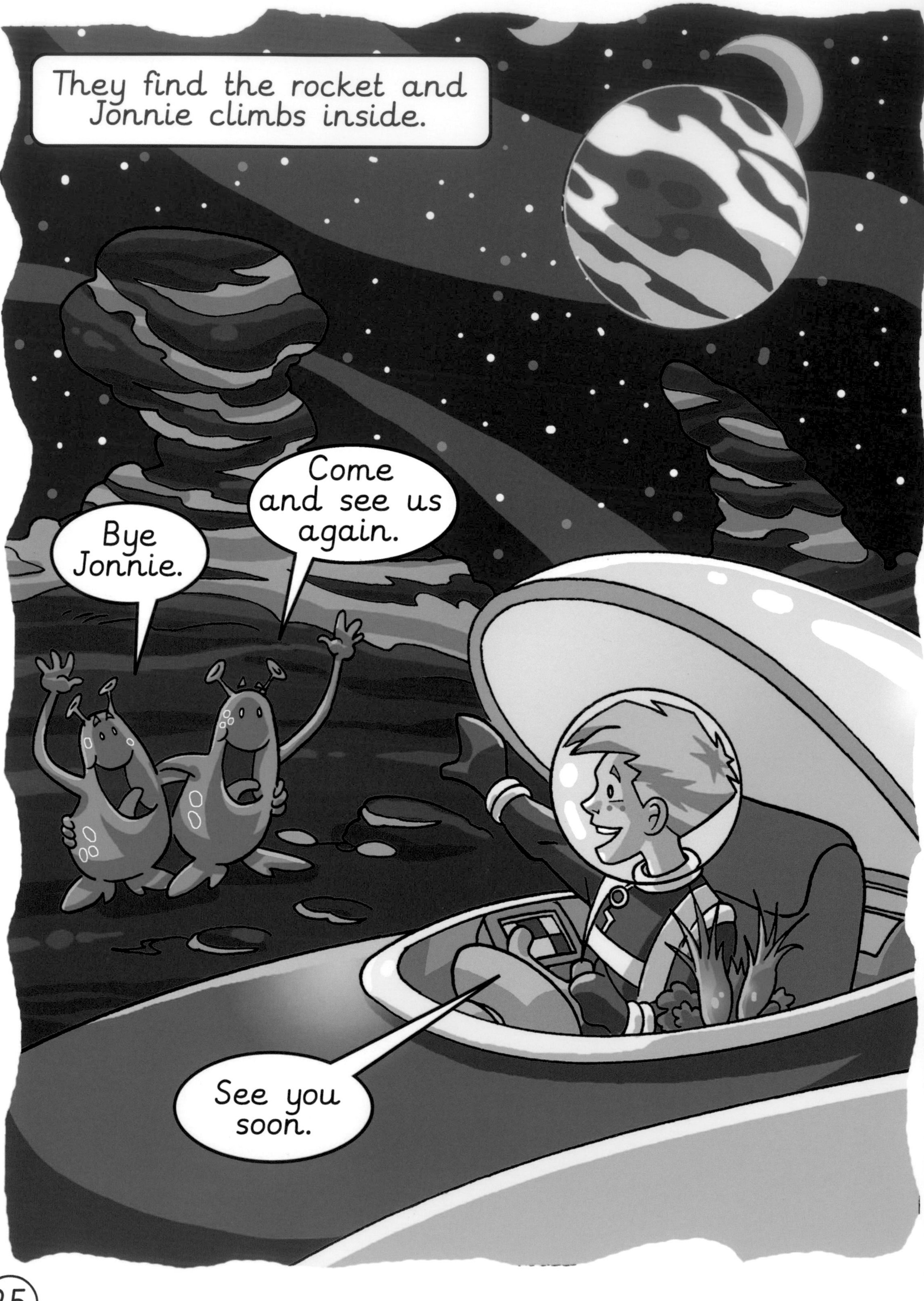
They find the rocket and Jonnie climbs inside.
Bye Jonnie.
Come and see us again.
See you soon.

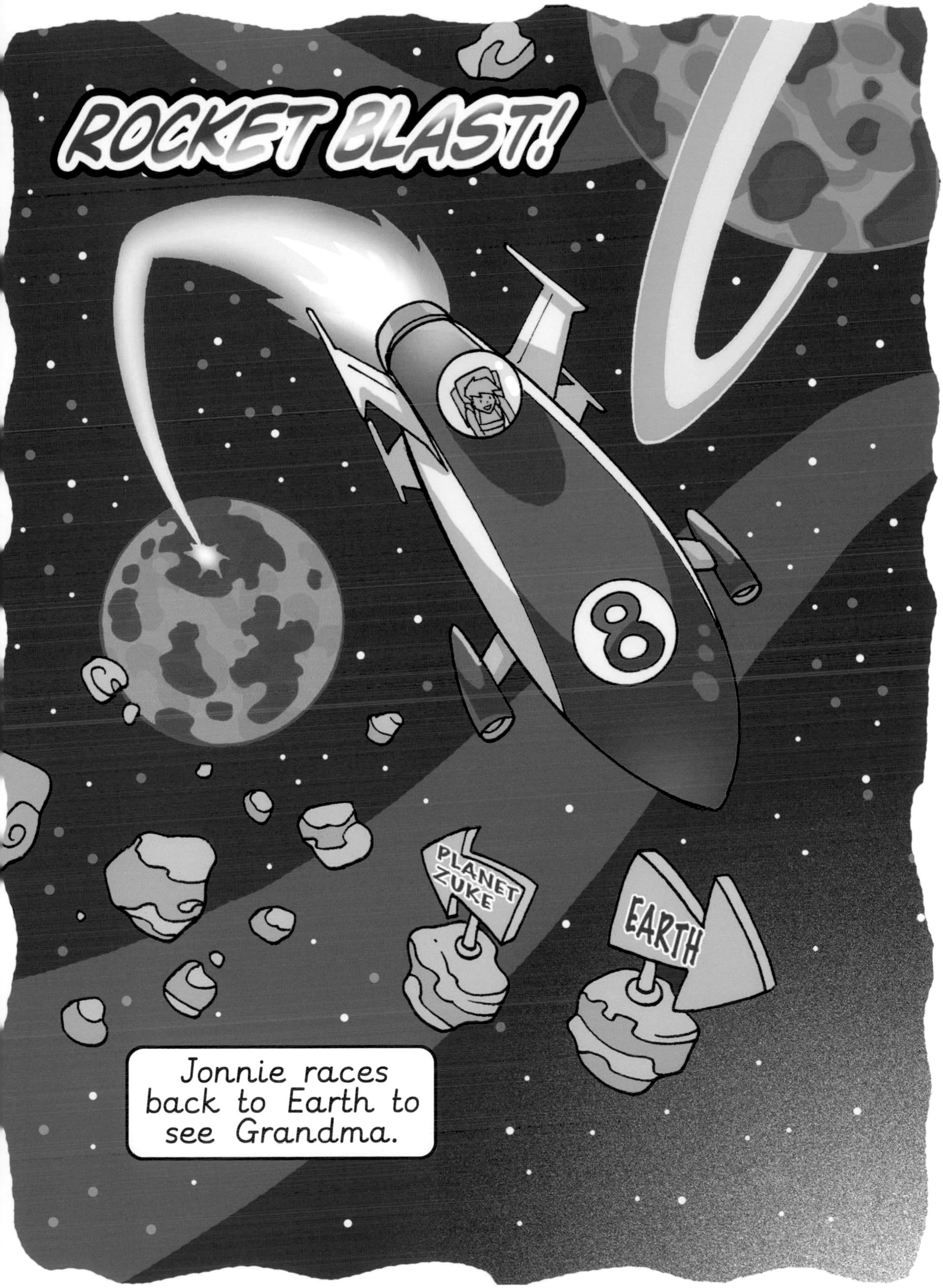
ROCKET BLAST!
PLANET ZUKE
EARTH
Jonnie races back to Earth to see Grandma.

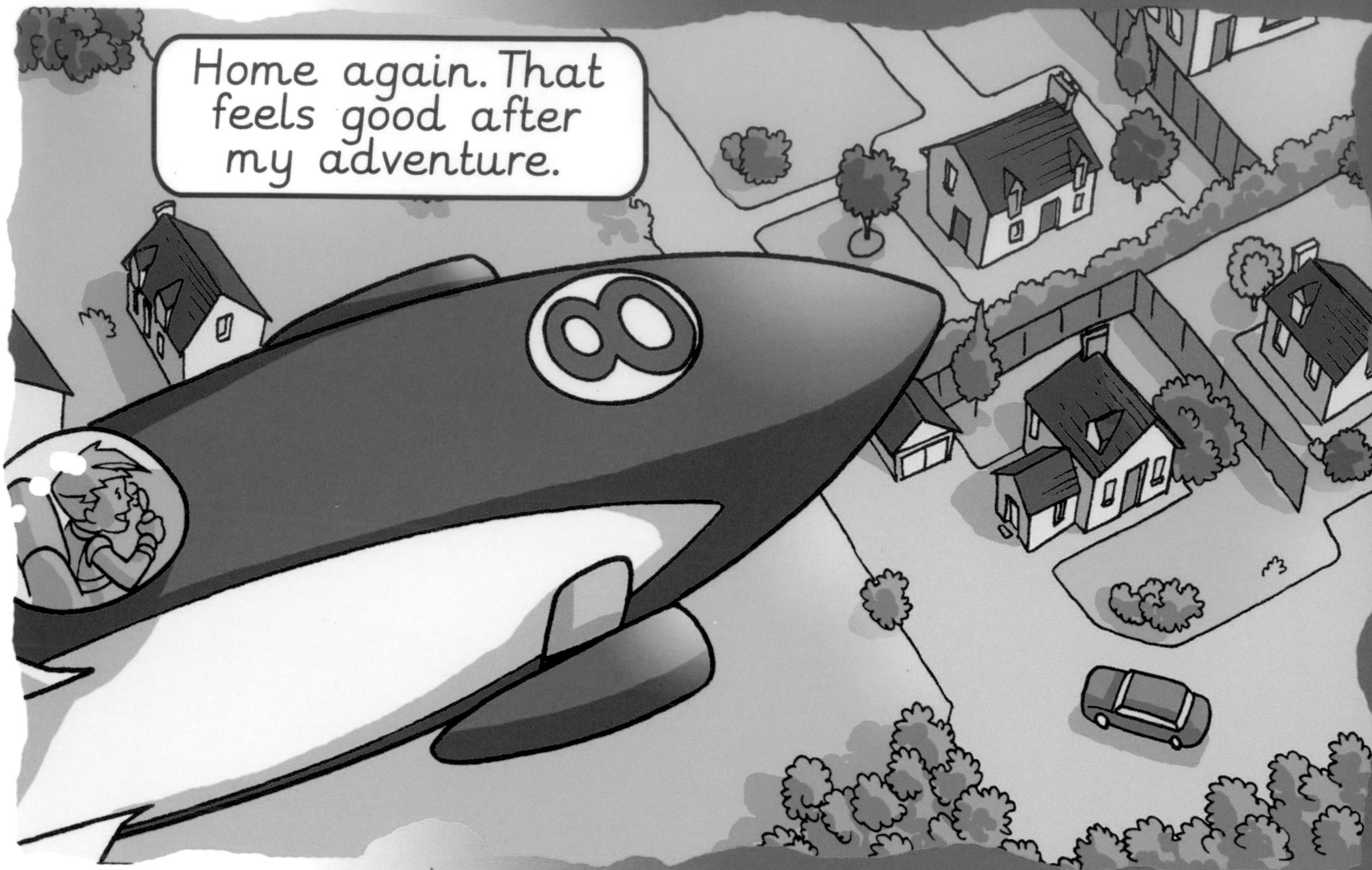
Home again. That feels good after my adventure.

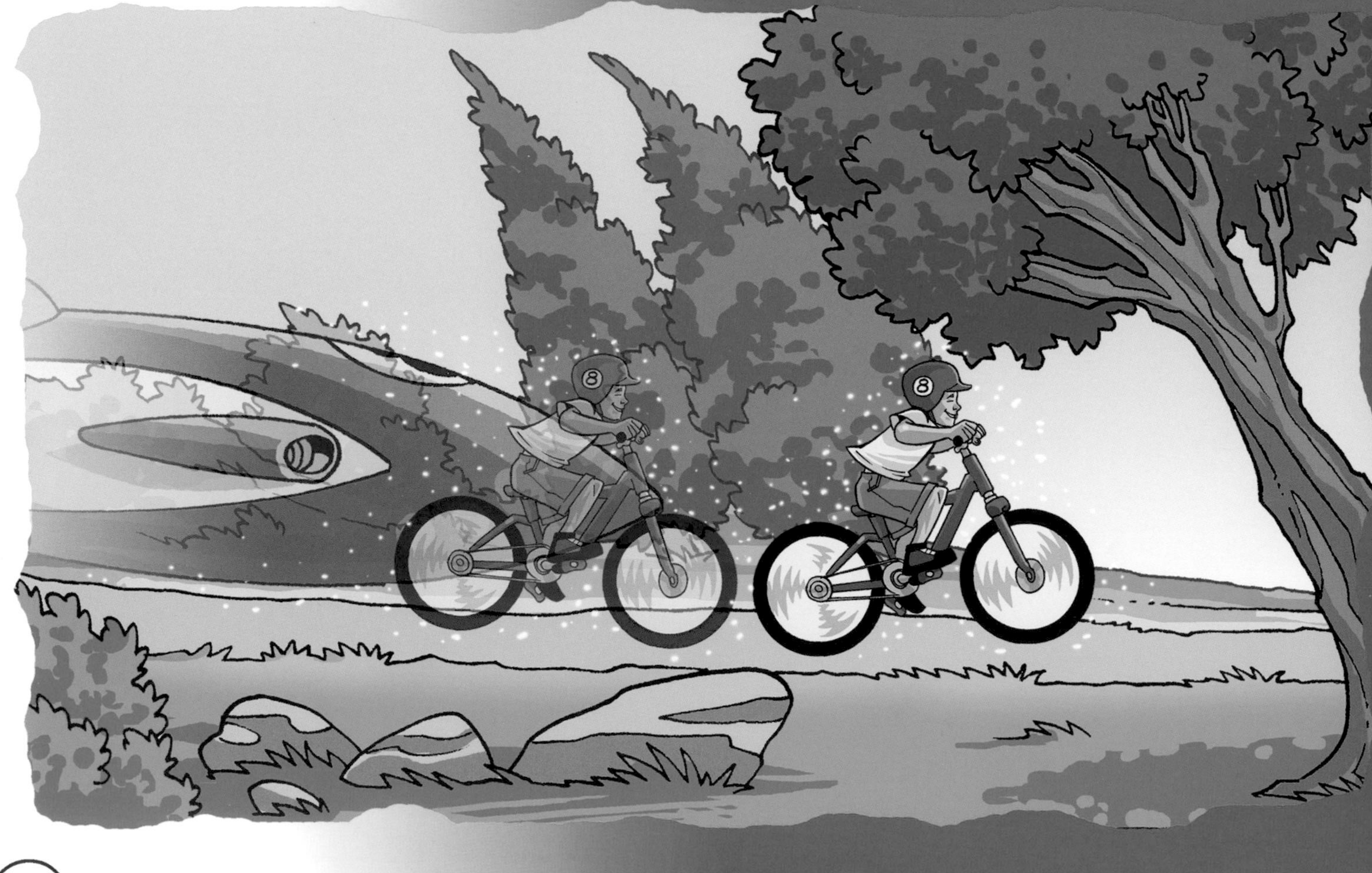

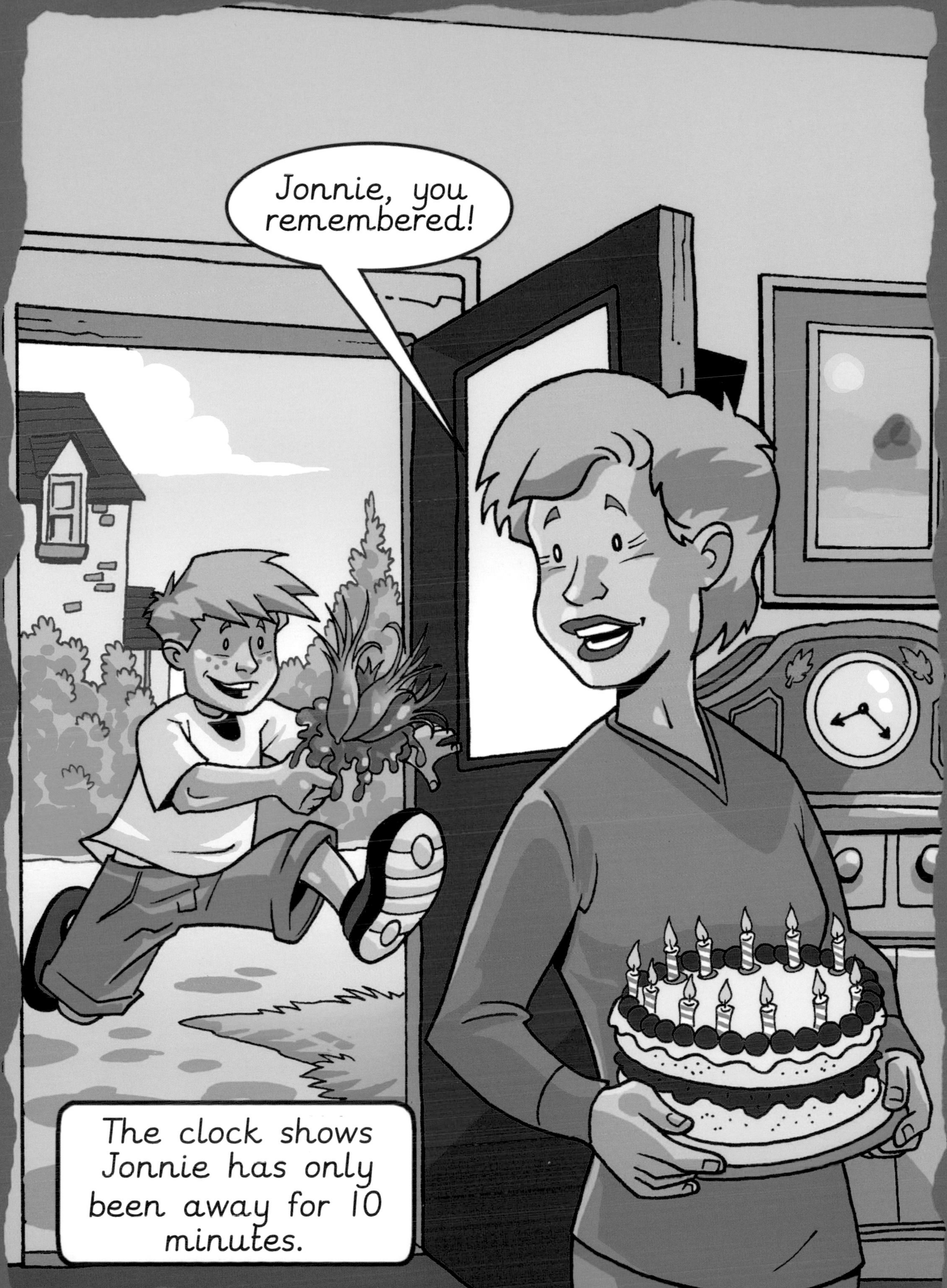
Jonnie, you remembered!
The clock shows Jonnie has only been away for 10 minutes.

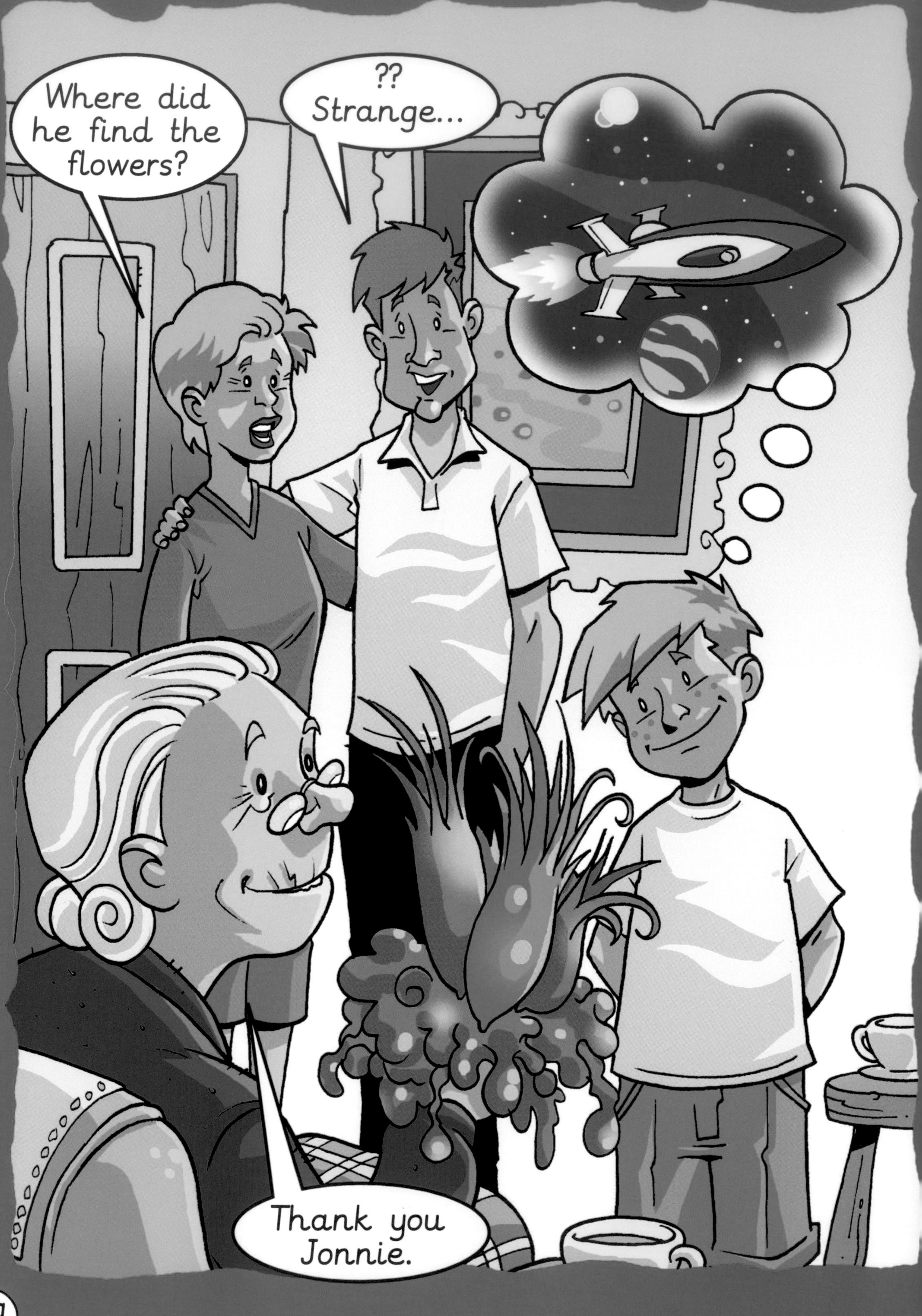
Where did he find the flowers?
??
Strange...
Thank you Jonnie.

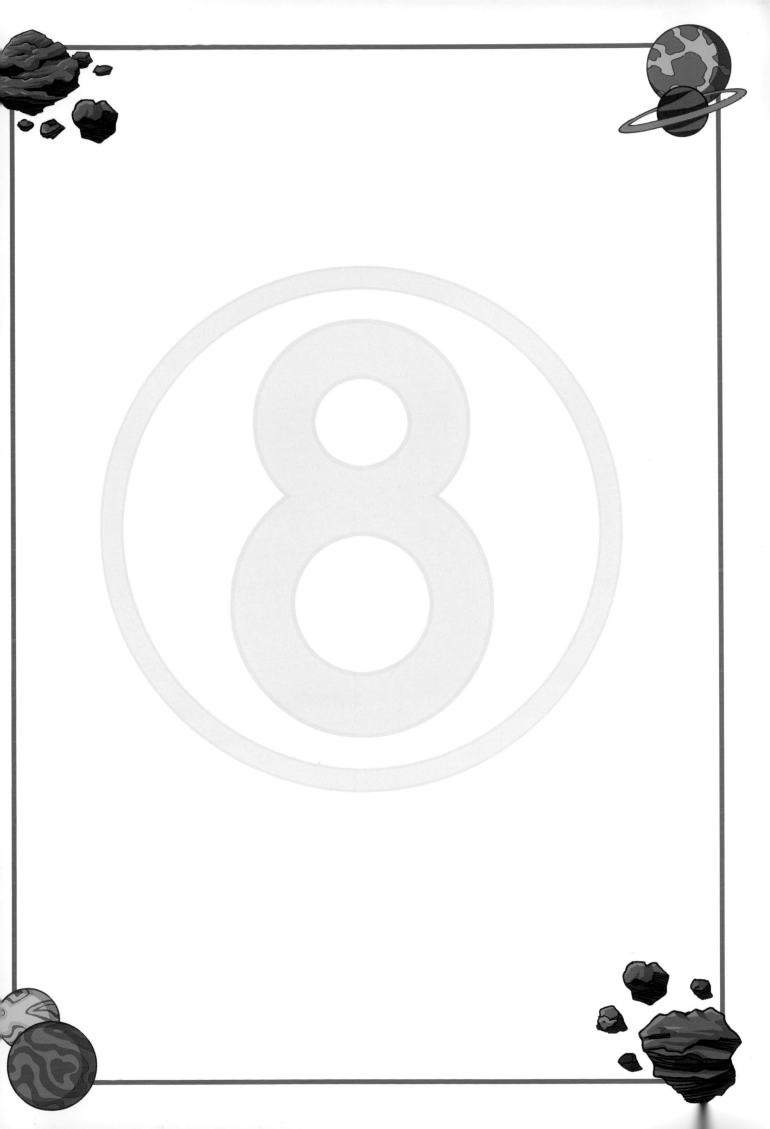

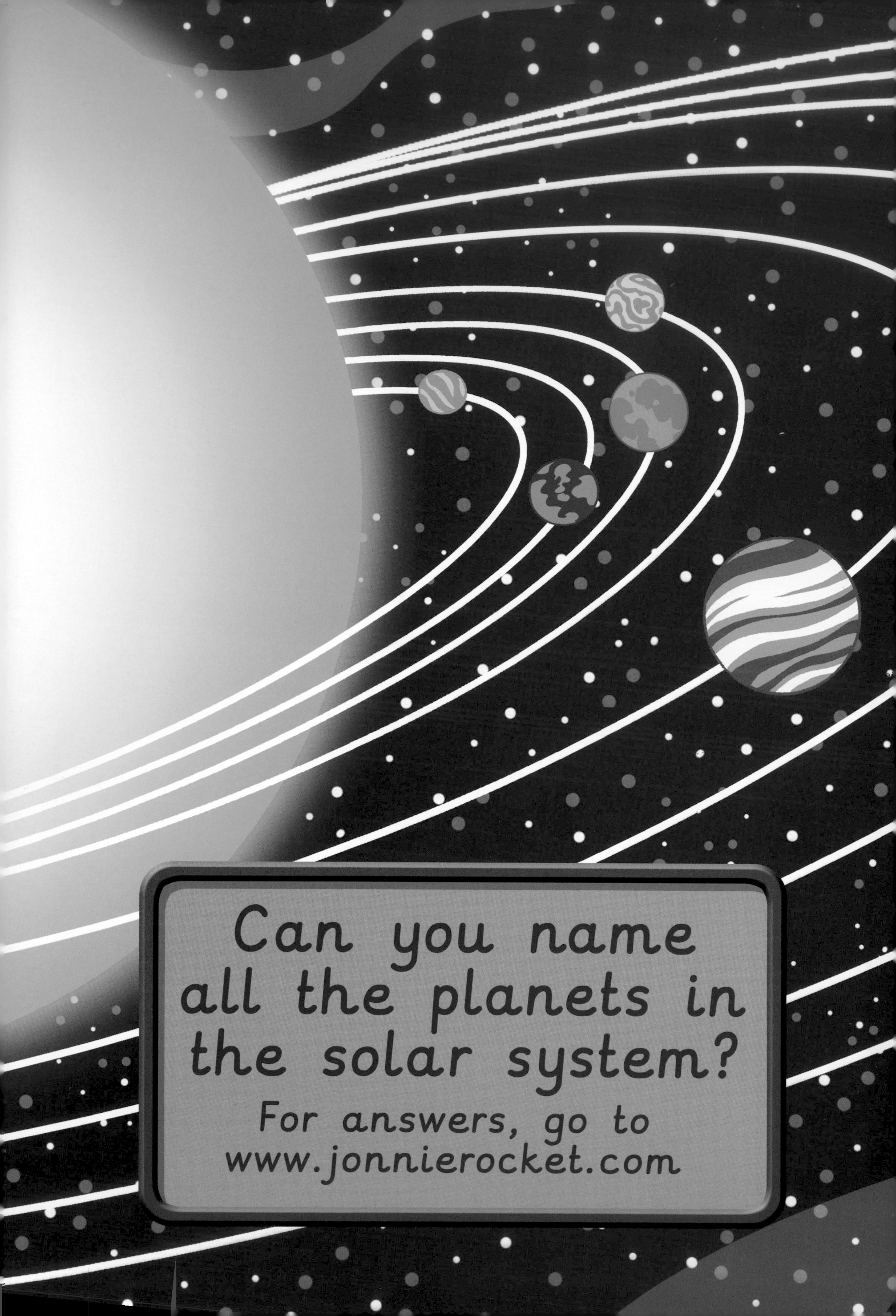
Can you name all the planets in the solar system?
For answers, go to www.jonnierocket.com

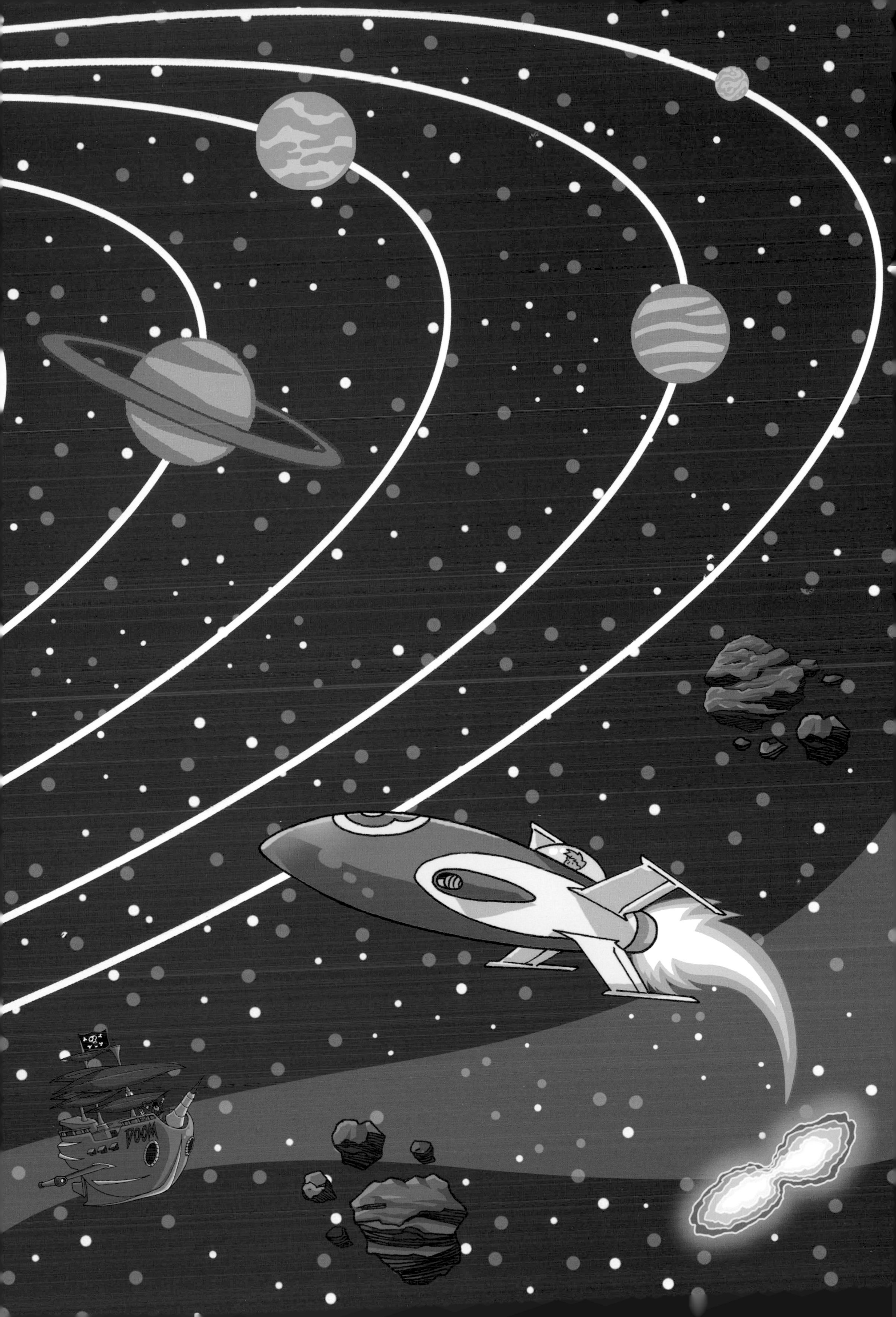
DOOM

About the Author
John Chapman – Creator, Author

As a young boy, the wonder of the universe and a love of
cycling had always been close to John's heart. Growing up in the 1960s John
had begun to form the first concepts of an idea through his strong imagination
and creative role-playing. He dreamt of rocket-ships and space adventures, and
was passionate about his bicycle and the escapism it gave him. Therefore it was
no surprise that in 1998 John had the idea for his imaginary character
Jonnie Rocket.

With the creation of this character firmly embedded in John's
imagination he spent the next two years formulating the idea; compiling the
draft of his first book 'The Adventures of Jonnie Rocket' in the year 2000.
He wrote this initial book as a scripted storyboard, with the aim of animating
the character of Jonnie Rocket as a TV series.

John has since created a collection of stories, centred on 'The Adventures of
Jonnie Rocket', twelve of which will be published in book form.

As part of John's imaginary space adventure, it was with some irony that in
1976 he found himself making a brief appearance as an X-Wing pilot in 'Star
Wars (A New Hope)', living out the dream of a space adventurer through the
most iconic sci-fi film of all time! Bringing Jonnie Rocket to life after four
decades must surely be John Chapman's intention....

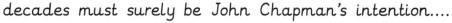

The Adventures of Jonnie Rocket: Books in the Series

THE ADVENTURES OF
JONNIE ROCKET
JOHN CHAPMAN

THE ADVENTURES OF JONNIE ROCKET

ISBN: 978-0-9573035-0-8

Jonnie, aged 8, battles with Space Pirates and visits Zuke, a very strange planet.

THE ADVENTURES OF
JONNIE ROCKET
SAGA. 1
JOHN CHAPMAN

SAGA 1: THE RIDE OF TERROR

ISBN: 978-0-9573035-2-2

Jonnie, now aged 12, is on a mission to save the school bus. Will he succeed, or have the bullies gone too far this time?

THE ADVENTURES OF
JONNIE ROCKET
SAGA. 2
JOHN CHAPMAN

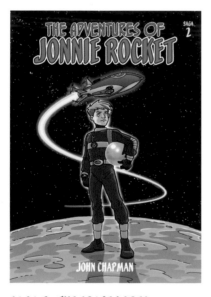

SAGA 2: THE SPACE LOBES

ISBN: 978-0-9573035-1-5

Jonnie crashes on Planet Cranium and meets the alien Space Lobes.

THE ADVENTURES OF
JONNIE ROCKET
SAGA. 3
JOHN CHAPMAN

SAGA 3: THE SEA OF SARGOSS

ISBN: 978-0-9573035-3-9

Dr Avatar sends Jonnie to Sargoss, which is facing an ecological disaster of devastating proportions. Can he save the universe?

Become a Rocketeer: visit www.jonnierocket.com and learn more about Jonnie's world!